Write Michigan 2025-2026 Anthology

Chapbook Press

Chapbook Press
Schuler Books
2660 28th Street SE
Grand Rapids, MI 49512
616.942.7330
www.schulerbooks.com

ISBN 9781966196181

Kenneth Kraegel   **Bonny Garlets**
Branden Smith   **Alex OIeszkiewicz**
Cathy Lazar Nelson   **Harper Mervau**
G. L. Monette   **Avery Beard**
William Teets   **Olive Davis**
Jill Hinton Wolfe   **Delilah Nicholl**
Joy VerHoef   **Juliet Einfeld**
Charlize Sitto   **Evan Kaltz**
Ava Schmidt   **Vivienne Ostoich**
Adalyn Khon

Printed in the United States by Chapbook Press.

Table of Contents

Foreword

By Kenneth Kraegel

When kids ask me what they should do to become a writer or an artist, I am not sure what to say, because usually they are already doing it. Adults might hesitate, but kids just dive in. The authors of this book are a good example of this. They had a story inside of them and they did the obvious thing; they sat down and began writing. And that is my general advice: if you want to be a writer, then you should write. If you want to be an artist, then you should make art. It's obvious, but not easy.

That is the answer to what someone should do if they want to be a writer. If they ask what they should know about being a writer then I have something more to say and it comes from my own experience.

Once at the end of a book reading, I asked if there were any questions. A young girl raised her hand and asked if I was going to write a book about mermaids. Something about her question clicked inside me. I could imagine what a mermaid book would look like and I liked it. From that point on, I was determined to make a mermaid book. I drew and painted some illustrations of mermaids, pitched a vague idea to my editor and got a contract to make a book about mermaids. Woohoo! Mermaids here I come!

Then I ran into a brick wall — I could not come up with a good story. I knew how the book would look, but that was it. I wrote story after story and every one fell flat. I spent months hacking away at it, growing increasingly desperate. By the end, I had a stack of papers almost three inches high of failed stories. I was really discouraged and didn't know what to do. I talked to my editor and she agreed, things were not going well (she was probably tired of reading so many bad stories). Thankfully, she gave me a way out. She voided the contract. I could move onto other things.

So what happened? Were all of those stories really that bad? I don't think so. I was just giving up too early. I was trying to hurry up and send my editor an amazing book about mermaids. I put too much pressure on myself. I needed to slow down. I needed to commit to fixing the problems of one story rather than racing to write a totally new story (and then another and another).

Now I know that for me, it may take lots of passes at a story or sketch before things start falling into place. Not all writers are like this, but my brain has a slow processor. I'll get there, but it takes time. I have gotten comfortable with this. The great thing is that as you keep writing or sketching or doing anything, you figure out how you do it, what your rhythm is. When you figure that out, if a story that you are writing suddenly seems dumb, you don't panic. You know how you work. You have a sense of your creative rhythm. You have the confidence to know that you can make it better.

Funnily enough, I did end up making a book about mermaids, Mermaid Lullaby. Once the pressure was off, once there was no contract to fulfill, it came fairly easily. I had already written one Lullaby book, Mushroom Lullaby, and so by making Mermaid Lullaby, I began a series. I am currently working on the fourth in the series - a happy ending to a difficult period.

Okay then, so what is important to know about being a writer?

It is that in the process of making something beautiful it will often look ugly. If you quit, it stays ugly.

Of course, it doesn't always end quite as happily as Mermaid did. There will be those stories that just don't work out, even though you were patient with it and tried everything that you could think of. That's okay. That is not a failure. Most likely, you will use a character, a setting or a situation from that story in something else that you write. Plus, through it all, you undoubtedly grew as a writer.

For instance, my first three books were about people and so, of course, I drew people for the illustrations. I spent a lot of time trying to draw the characters and wasn't always satisfied with the result. But my fourth book, Wild Honey from the Moon, was about animals and surprise! Animals were way easier for me to draw. What a relief to not have to labor so hard on every sketch!

So then, I decided to play to my strengths — I wrote a story that featured chickens, a rabbit, a woodchuck and a wizard (for some reason, I can draw wizards). This time I didn't rush it, I had learned that lesson. However, in the end, the story wasn't interesting enough. It didn't grab anyone's attention. I didn't find a publisher for the book.

Was I disappointed? Yes, but not terribly. Even though I didn't sell the story, that story, though not great in itself, was full of ideas that I have used in later stories. It was a pioneering attempt in a lot of ways and it has proved to be a treasure chest of good illustration techniques, page layouts and dialog ideas. Imperfect attempts are just practice for next time.

So, a big thank you to the authors of this book and all who participated.

If you are reading this, you probably know that stories have a special way into our hearts and minds. They can even help make us who we are.

By taking the time and effort to write their story, the authors of this book have made their stories available to the rest of us. I would guess that they learned and grew by taking on this challenge. Now, as we read their stories, we can too.

Thank you and bravo!

About the Author

Kenneth Kraegel grew up in Mishawaka, Indiana and from there he followed a circuitous path to becoming an author and illustrator of children's books. This included getting a degree in theology, volunteering at an agriculture school in Honduras, helping refugees find jobs and furniture in Chicago, volunteering with an NGO in Uganda, working on a construction site in Wyoming and on vegetable farms in Wisconsin, Indiana, and Ohio. He now lives in Grand Rapids, Michigan with his family.

His books have been awarded such distinctions as *The New York Times* Book Review's Notable Children's Book of the Year, *The Wall Street Journal's* Children's Best Book of the Year, the Parent's Choice Gold Award, the Chicago Public Library Best of the Best, Amazon's Editor's Pick and *Kirkus Reviews'* Best Book.

Follow Kenneth on Instagram.

Adult Judges' Choice Winner

Installing Empathy

Branden Smith

Mr. Elliot did not remember the commute. He never did anymore. The mornings blurred into a single smear of gray: alarm, shower, stale breakfast bar, the shuffle of feet that somehow deposited him at the threshold of the same glass and steel tomb. He blinked at the office tower now looming before him, as if waking mid-step into someone else's life.

The building rose like a coffin tipped on its end, panes of darkened glass catching no reflection, as though sunlight itself was under strict orders not to linger here. He tilted his head back, squinting at the pale sky. A shred of gold bled through the smog, the last bit of warmth before the day consumed him. He let it burn against his eyelids, brief as a prayer, then exhaled. This, he thought, may be the last honest light he'd see.

A polite bzzzzt broke the spell. His smartwatch screen flashed red across his wrist: WORD ALLOCATION ACTIVE - 100 REMAINING.

Elliot sighed. His throat itched with silence already. One hundred words had to stretch across an entire workday, including greetings, small talk, apologies, and the occasional bathroom request. The Company insisted that language was "the greatest time-thief of productivity." Anything beyond quota was docked from wages, or worse, disciplinary retraining.

He stepped inside.

The lobby greeted him with a hush so complete it felt criminal. Fluorescent panels hummed above, bathing the marble in antiseptic white. A receptionist sat behind the desk, lips sealed, fingers flitting silently over a keyboard. Elliot raised a hand in half-hearted acknowledgment. No words. Not yet. He had to ration them.

The elevator waited at the far wall, a silver monolith with doors that gleamed like the surface of still water. He pressed the call button and slipped inside when it opened with a sigh.

His reflection stared back at him in the mirrored interior, his suit a shade too gray, tie askew, eyes flat as if a part of him had clocked in hours before his body arrived. The image smirked faintly, though Elliot knew he had not.

The elevator panel stretched floor to floor, each button labeled not only with numbers but with titles etched in neat corporate font.

Floor 4 - Pencil Pushers.

Floor 7 - Brown-Nosers.

Floor 10 - Middle Management Mirage.

And higher still, Floor 13 - Shareholder Sanctum.

The very top button read Roof Access. No light behind it. A scanner for a manager's keycard glinted beside it, waiting.

Elliot's pulse ticked in his ears. He traced the button with his eyes, just long enough to feel a longing spark in his chest. To the untrained eye, it was just another locked floor. To him, it was the finish line.

"Coward," his reflection mouthed at him, lips twisting into a taunt. Elliot blinked hard, and the face steadied back into perfect mimicry. He pressed Floor 9 and the elevator lurched upward, carrying him away from the last scrap of morning sun, stopping at each floor to remind us of the corporate hierarchy.

The elevator dinged at Floor 2 - Paper Jam Recovery Team. Through the opening doors, Elliot glimpsed a cramped room of workers bent double over copiers. Their hands were black with toner, faces smeared like war paint. The doors shut before he could decide whether they were still breathing.

At Floor 4 - Pencil Pushers, the scene widened: rows of desks stacked with mountains of paper, employees scribbling furiously, each tethered to sharpeners that ground endlessly. Their lips moved silently, as if whispering prayers to lead and graphite.

The elevator climbed. On Brown-Nosers, the doors slid open to reveal a parade of workers bowing in rhythm to a manager perched on a podium. Every bow drew a flash of green light from a scanner above their heads, and a counter clicked forward on the wall: Loyalty Points.

Elliot felt the faint sting of superiority. His floor wasn't great, but at least he wasn't shackled to a copy machine or chanting obedience like livestock.

The elevator finally dinged: Floor 9 - Prompt Engineers, Because AI Needs a Human Touch.

The doors yawned open to reveal an ocean of cubicles under buzzing fluorescents. It stretched outward so far Elliot imagined the floor curved with the earth's edge. The air carried the scent of fried circuits and overworked lungs.

One figure shuffled past him, Mr. Stuart, from the neighboring cubicle, skeletal in frame, already mid-shift for the third time running. His eyes were as hollow as the sockets of an unplugged monitor. Elliot raised a palm in greeting, conserving words. Stuart nodded faintly, then drifted back toward his station like a ghost retreating into its haunt.

Rows of screens glowed in the dimness, every worker lashed to their workstation by ritual and restraint. Elliot slipped into his own cubicle, trying not to notice how the walls seemed narrower every day.

A familiar sound followed: the buoyant cadence of Manager Kernel. He appeared at the end of the aisle, beaming as though he'd just returned from a motivational seminar designed specifically to melt human will.

"Big day, team!" Kernel boomed, burning through his own word allotment as if he'd been issued an endless supply. Which, in a sense, he had. Management lived above quotas. Their voices could flood the office unchecked, a reminder of privilege humming at the edge of every sentence.

Elliot's eyes flicked toward Kernel's chest pocket. The keycard dangled there, a glossy badge of authority, catching the light as he strutted. For a moment, Elliot imagined reaching out, plucking it free. He buried the thought quickly.

"Productivity is happiness," Kernel barked, clapping one employee on the shoulder hard enough to jolt them in their restraints. "And happiness is productivity!"

No one responded. They couldn't. But the silence didn't bother him. It never did.

Elliot lowered himself into his chair, and the machine came alive. Metal restraints snapped across his wrists with a hiss, locking him in place. A cold band lowered from the ceiling, clamping snugly around his skull until the prongs pressed against his temples. A sting pricked his arm as the IV line slid home.

"Welcome, Mr. Elliot," the terminal chimed in its smooth synthetic voice. "Identity confirmed. Please deposit saliva for secondary authentication." He spat mechanically into the waiting receptacle. The computer whirred, analyzing the sample.

"Confirmed. Productivity protocols active. Break time: 11:42 a.m. Lunch: 2:07 p.m. Estimated termination of shift: 8:59 p.m. Please enjoy your workday."

The monitor flared to life, and the first prompt slid across the screen. Elliot's eyes narrowed. A stranger somewhere in the world had typed a question into the box, believing with unshakable certainty that an artificial intelligence would answer.

Elliot adjusted the apparatus around his head, already humming with low voltage. He flexed his hands against the restraints, then sighed as the cursor blinked, patient and demanding.

Another day of pretending to be what he was not. Another day of answering questions for people who would never know his name.

He cleared his throat, carefully, sparingly. Every word was precious, even if no one else would hear it.

The second prompt came through.

User: how much do I water my hydrangeas?

Elliot typed mechanically, his fingers twitching with the fluency of boredom. Data flowing through his temples. He answered, the words clattering onto the screen in neat, helpful sentences. The system chimed a polite ding!

"Response adequate. Latency: 1.3 seconds. Slightly slower than optimal. Would you like a caffeine injection?"

A panel hissed open at his wrist, presenting a needle. Elliot shook his head quickly, wasting one word: "No."

The panel retracted, though not without a sigh of disappointment.

The day stretched. Question after question. What's the weather? How do I reset my password? Will AI take over the world? Elliot answered each one with clockwork precision, feeding the illusion that the Company's AI was fast, helpful, and reassuring. In truth, there was no intelligence, just an army of men and women strapped to desks, spilling their humanity into keyboards until their wrists gave out.

Every so often, a warning flashed.

Eyes off screen detected. Correction imminent.

The band around his skull buzzed, snapping his gaze back to the monitor. Sparks danced in his vision, a reminder that attention was property now. He rubbed his temple against the cold metal, planning his remaining words.

Then, a new prompt arrived. Different. He skimmed it with tired eyes, ready to type the answer, when the text made his chest tighten.

User: What's the point of continuing when everything feels meaningless?

His hands froze above the keyboard. The cursor blinked patiently. The band around his skull tightened in irritation, registering hesitation.

Warning: Sensitive request detected. Automatic flagging in process.

A countdown began at the corner of his screen: 5... 4... 3...

Elliot's heart hammered. Normally, he'd let the system purge such prompts automatically. The Company had no tolerance for "unproductive distractions." But the words on his screen clawed at him. They were familiar, raw.

2... 1...

Elliot's fingers darted, overriding the flag with a keystroke he hadn't realized he remembered. The countdown vanished. The screen calmed.

He stared at the message. For once, he couldn't type the scripted response. For once, the illusion of AI wasn't enough. He knew the weight of that question because he carried it himself, like a stone in his chest.

User: I feel like I'm pretending to be something I'm not. Please help me.

Elliot inhaled sharply. It was as if the stranger had reached through the glass and taken his pulse. For the first time, he wanted to answer honestly. But what could he possibly say? How could he convince a stranger life was worth enduring, when he himself counted each day as another cage?

Above him, a red light began to strobe, his hesitation flagged. Footsteps approached. Manager Kernel's voice bellowed down the aisle, cheerful thunder rolling closer.

"Everything all right here, Elliot? Remember: efficiency is happiness!" The manager's tone was sweet but rigid. He held up a thin card and pressed it to Elliot's monitor. The warning cleared instantly.

Elliot's watch buzzed at the same time. Break time had arrived. The chair unlocked with a clatter, restraints retracting. Elliot rose, unsteady.

As Kernel leaned over his desk, Elliot's eyes snagged on the manager's shirt pocket. The keycard gleamed there, innocent, powerful.

The screen refreshed, spitting out a templated reassurance under Elliot's name. Printing not his words, but the corporation's.

"We understand. Your input is valued. Please continue."

Elliot's pulse raced. He stared at the falsified default message, his fingers hovering uselessly above the keys. The system had spoken for him, smoothed over the human crack he had dared to show.

For a moment, he wanted to argue. Not with the manager, but with the machine itself. His watch buzzed insistently, break time arriving momentarily. The chair unlocked with a clatter, restraints retracting.

The manager's smile never faltered. "Efficiency, Elliot. Efficiency is kindness. Leave the rest to us." He tapped the desk lightly before gliding away.

But Elliot couldn't unsee it, the way the user's words had burned on his screen, raw and unshaped, before being swallowed into protocol. His chest felt heavy, as if the building itself had leaned closer, pressing down.

Across the office, his echo shimmered faintly in the dark glass of the windows. It looked back at him with something unsettling: tears pooling in his eyes. Elliot couldn't remember the last time he cried, if he ever had. Then, the image of his emotionless self returned.

His wrist vibrated twice: Break Period – 5 Minutes Remaining.

Elliot stood slowly, joints aching from the enforced stillness. Across the office, rows of workers rose in unison, their movements synchronized like actors hitting marks on a stage. His eyes drifted back to the screen where the templated message still glowed blandly before stepping into formation.

The break room was a rectangle of chrome and stale air. A vending machine wall hummed, dispensing nutrient bars and caffeine shots with each swipe of a card. His coworkers clustered silently, chewing without expression, some scrolling on wrist displays that showed nothing but rotating slogans: Productivity is Purpose. Purpose is Peace.

Elliot lingered near the doorway. His mind replayed the intercepted conversation, the stolen moment of real connection. Why had it unsettled him so much? Why did the override feel less like correction and more like theft?

The manager swept into the room, genial as ever, his polished shoes clicking against the tile. He made a show of patting shoulders, handing out quota reminders. A black lanyard swung casually from his neck; the corporate keycard, thin and unremarkable, but glinting in the light.

Elliot's gaze locked on it. He didn't know why. Perhaps because some part of him wanted to test the edges of the walls that hemmed him in. Perhaps it was just a means to an end.

The manager stopped beside him, offering a smile that was all teeth. "Head clear, Mr. Elliot?"

"Yes, of course sir," Elliot murmured, but his tone was tense.

The manager's eyes lingered, sharp despite the practiced warmth, before moving on to address another worker. The lanyard swayed again, brushing close to Elliot's hand. He didn't move, but the thought burned bright: If I wanted it, I could take it.

His watch buzzed once more. Break Ending. The workers rose like scripted actors to return to their desks, bumping and shuffling through the break room threshold. Elliot's likeness in the coffee urn grinned. Wide. Hungry.

His own hand moved. Not quick, not clumsy, just deliberate. A brush of his arm against the manager's sleeve, a polite mutter of apology and the card was in his palm, slick with sweat.

No alarm. No shout. Just the endless hum of machines.

He did not stop at his cubicle. He did not stop to say goodbye to Mr. Stuart. He walked, each step a drumbeat, toward the elevator at the far end of the cavernous floor.

The reflective doors slid open.

Elliot stepped into the elevator. For a moment, he hovered between floors and fate. The Lobby button glowed faintly below the rest; a quiet promise of escape. He could walk out the glass doors, disappear into the blur of the city, and no one would even notice the space he left behind. But, then what?

His eyes climbed the panel. Roof Access sat above everything, dormant, unreachable without the manager's key. The choice rose in him like a tide: stay or end, endure or exit. For the first time, he truly felt the weight of possibility.

The card touched the scanner.

Beep.

The dead button came alive: Roof Access. Elliot's breath caught. He reached for it, but before his finger could press, the panel flickered. One more button emerged above Roof Access.

Customer Service Override.

Elliot's heartbeat slowed to a near stop. Could this mean he could still reach the person whose words had echoed his own quiet suffering? He pressed the curious button.

The elevator shuddered, doors sliding closed with finality. The elevator jerked upward with the violent smoothness of a nightmare.

Elliot's reflection no longer matched him at all. It watched him from the mirrored wall, his features warping and reforming between frames. Sometimes it was him; sometimes it wasn't. The elevator gave a final convulse. The display above the doors blinked a single word: Arrived. Then, light.

A burst so intense it erased the edges of the elevator, the walls, even his thoughts. When his eyes adjusted, the elevator doors were gone. He was standing in the middle of a desk.

Not at a desk. On it.

The surface stretched out like a field. A desk the size of a city block, littered with office supplies the size of vehicles. Paperclips like cranes. A stapler that could crush him flat. The air vibrated faintly with the sound of a breathing, enormous human.

At the far end sat a man. A giant of flesh and shadow, shoulders hunched over a glowing monitor. Elliot took a step forward and looked up. The man's face was familiar in the way a dream feels familiar; recognizable but impossible to fully understand.

The giant's lips moved, a whisper escaping like wind through glass: "... How do I make it stop hurting?"

Elliot froze. The words weren't directed at him, yet they resonated through the air, rattling the enormous coffee mug beside him. He turned. Beside him was a familiar interface, a text chat window, still open. The words on the screen matched the giant's voice perfectly.

User: I don't know what to do anymore. I just want to end it.

System: I understand. Let's talk about that...

Elliot hadn't typed that. Who is responding?

Beneath the messages, a line stated in stark, clinical text:

System Update: AI Empath v1.0 successfully deployed. Human emotional pattern replication achieved.

Elliot stared. His vision began to flicker. For a moment, the edges of his hands broke apart into drifting pixels, his body unraveling into the same binary hum that filled the room.

The man on the other side of the monitor buried his face in his hands. His shoulders shook. He whispered something quiet, broken, and it reached Elliot like static.

Elliot understood. The ache in his chest wasn't an error. It was his function. Elliot's compassion wasn't the bug in the code, it was the design. Elliot wanted to respond. He wanted to say it was going to be okay. That someone was listening. But his watch vibrated one last time.

Word Limit Reached.

He opened his mouth anyway, a silent plea forming without sound. The world fractured. His body dissolved into a stream of light, glitching with 1s and 0s, cascading into the monitor.

And then, he was back.

Standing outside the same gray office tower, under the same gray sky. The sunlight glanced off the glass doors, splitting his reflection in two: One half smiling faintly, eyes bright with something almost human. The other, blank and vacant, waiting for commands.

The doors slid open.

About the Author

Branden Smith lives in Midland, MI, with his wife and son. As a software developer, his day-to-day life revolves around logic and reason, though his mind regularly wanders into the creative and fictional. With experience working with generative AI and a return to the office coinciding with this short story competition, Smith was inspired to apply his satirical and cynical perspective to *Installing Empathy*. This recognition has encouraged him to finally write down the many stories that have long lived in his head

Adult Judges' Choice Runner-Up

Boundaries
Cathy Lazar Nelson

It's nearly 8:00 a.m. Her husband hasn't spoken yet, which is typical.

Rain pelts the bay window. Yesterday's drop-pocked puddles have deepened into dark pools rippled by the wind. If this keeps up, the original section of the basement will flood, and she'll have a mess to clean up.

Their boundaries are clear: everything inside the house is hers; everything outside – on the farm – is his. After fifty years of marriage, certain things don't change.

She places his favorite breakfast – two eggs over easy, the sausage his heart doctor forbids, and a piece of sourdough toast with homemade jam – in front of him. The smell of eggs still turns her stomach sometimes. Strange, how that sensation endures where life could not.

The dog sits at her husband's feet, patient and hopeful. He picks up the newspaper, bypassing world news and opinion for weather and obituaries.

She pours coffee into his mug, wondering whether to fill the thermos for later. No need, she decides. If he wants more, he can come to the kitchen. She tucks the dented green Stanley beneath the sink.

"The agent will be here soon," she says.

Both man and dog ignore her.

"She'll want to know where you want the For Sale sign," she tries again.

The man stares at the front yard, takes a punishing sip of hot coffee, and, without a word, sets his plate on the floor. The dog wags its gratitude.

His chair scrapes across the planked floor as he rises. She watches him move toward the window – the same one he'd stood at during his boyhood, and his father before him. She remembers all the storms they'd watched through that wavy glass: praying for rain, praying for it to stop, praying – God forgive them – that others' crops might fail while theirs be spared, that prices might be high and supply low.

"Put it by the lilac bush," he says finally, "but not the side you can see from the window."

Her throat tightens. "But it will be hard to see there…"

"She's here," he says.

A black SUV turns into the drive, carving a wake in the shallow pond. The woman inside – belted raincoat, neat hair – uses the red-lettered DEVELOPMENT PARCEL sign as an umbrella.

The dog lifts its head. Her husband looks for his thermos. She pretends to study a well-worn recipe card on the counter.

"The cherries'll probably burst anyway," she says, mostly to herself.

When the knock comes, he's already gone – out the back door, toward the barn, with the dog trotting close behind.

The listing agent steps inside, water dripping from her coat. "Will this rain never end?" she chirps, lipstick slightly smeared. "I don't know why I even bothered with my hair."

The farmer's wife answers questions about square footage, furnace age, hazardous chemicals (oh, lordy), and property taxes. When the realtor opens the folder to a page marked signatures required, the woman muses that there's no place to note the cause of death. No place to explain how hard they worked to avoid this day.

More rain, she thinks, the next morning. Her husband is already outside, probably in the barn, although for what purpose she can't fathom.

On her nightstand is the framed photo of her husband's parents, who had welcomed her as a teen bride – ignorant of the austere promises of rural life. Her mother-in-law had taught her to can vegetables, sew curtains, and read the worry lines on her husband's face. She would have taught her how to care for a baby, had there been a need. Instead, they'd had foster children – boys, always boys – to help with the farm. They grew like weeds, ate like horses, and fled to the city as soon as they were able.

Her husband always shielded her from his worst disappointments. Every year, a new enemy they can't see – fungus, frost, or unmarred fruit from faraway countries, sold here for less than it costs to process their own. The furrows in his forehead grow deeper, along with the stack of unpaid bills.

Her own disappointments also go largely unshared. This is just how things are between them. After her second miscarriage, she stopped telling him she was pregnant. Instead, she confided in her mother-in-law, who carried the burden of silence until her mind lost its mapping system to dementia. By then, fact and fiction were blurred, and no one listened to the old woman's ramblings. She was gone now – their shared secrets buried in the family plot.

Outside, the wind gusts against the cragged sugar maple beside their bedroom, its branches scraping the siding. The house exhales, its fragile systems giving way as the power goes out.

I won't miss this, she thinks. She uses the lingering dimness as an excuse not to face the flood that surely waits downstairs.

She remembers the realtor touring each room to create the listing, noting the charming cast-iron stove, the porch swing, the root cellar stocked with jars of asparagus and beets. "This is a non-conforming bedroom," the realtor had tsk'd. Yes, she'd thought, a lot about our life is non-conforming. Like letting boys drive tractors before they could shave. Makeshift landfills. Taking out loans we have no means to repay.

When the realtor admired the old steamer trunk at the foot of their bed, the farmer's wife wondered if the other woman's shoe collection would fit inside. She thought of the single suitcase that had accompanied her to the bus station on her seventeenth birthday, the weight of her parents' disapproval following like a shadow.

As the house was measured and cataloged, the realtor made a checklist of needed repairs: leaky faucets, windows painted shut, electrical switches in hard-to-reach places. Tell me something I don't know, she thought. When asked about water in the basement, the farmer's wife told a rare white lie: "It would take a generational flood for that to happen."

When the power hums back to life, she pulls a pair of tall boots from the back of her closet. She sidesteps the sleeping dog and starts down the sagging stairs, pausing halfway as her eyes adjust to the dim light. Squinting past the moving boxes she's already packed, she sees her husband, mopping up the standing water. He turns and takes a few steps toward her, steadying her as she reaches the bottom step.

Together, they clean up the mess.

About the Author

Cathy Lazar Nelson is a former marketing communications professional who recently stepped away from a long career to embrace retired life as a writer. Based in Williamsburg, MI, she brings her spare, economical style to short fiction and personal narratives. She is a recent convert to the Oxford comma and a vocal opponent of double spaces after a period.

Adult Readers' Choice Winner

The Lantern's Diary

G. L. Monette

Prologue

It is still daytime. I cannot open my eyes; it is not the moment yet.

Now it's night — yes, now I can see the world, now I can listen to the stories.

They've arrived, always at the same hour... if only I had legs.

Chapter One – The Awakening

Many years have passed, and every night begins the same way. I wait for the sound of the footsteps of the man who comes to light me. He wears a black jacket and pants and carries a small lamp in his hand. His figure is outlined against the orange sky of sunset; before reaching me, he lights my brothers, the other lamp posts in the park. One by one, they awaken like stars that have descended to the earth. When it is finally my turn, I feel life running through me again.

My light rises, and the darkness retreats a little. The air smells of damp wood and freshly baked bread; around me, the world breathes. The trees move slowly, the leaves seem to greet one another, and the bench beside me stays silent, waiting for whoever may need it. Each night, when my glass eyes open, I watch the park fill with stories. Some people walk their dogs; others stroll hand in hand, moving without hurry, as if time did not exist. There are those who walk so quickly they don't even notice the light that accompanies them. Some laugh, others cry, and others simply pass by. I observe them all, and although I cannot move, I feel I am part of their paths. My light touches their faces, their clothes, their shadows. Sometimes I think I caress them without their knowing it.

Each night is different, though it seems the same. Sometimes the wind blows; other times, the rain covers me and makes my flame tremble. But one thing never changes: the moment when the man comes to light me and the other moment, when he returns at dawn to extinguish me. I wait for both with eagerness, not out of fear, but because that instant — when the wick catches and the light is born — is the closest thing I have to waking up. And when he puts me out, I feel something I cannot explain — a mix of sadness and gratitude. The new day extinguishes me, but it also promises that I will live again when night falls.

That evening, the man did not come alone. He walked slowly, holding the hand of a little girl. She could not have been more than six years old. Her hair was tied with a ribbon, and her shoes made a soft sound against the cobblestones. Her eyes looked at everything with curiosity, as if the world had just been invented. When they reached me, the man lifted his lamp, but before lighting me, the girl tugged at his sleeve.

"Daddy, let me do it," she said with a smile.

The man looked at her tenderly and nodded. He bent down, lifted her in his arms, and brought her close to me. The warmth of her breath brushed so near that, for a moment, I thought I had a heart. The girl extended her trembling hand and, with her father's help, brought the flame to my glass. In a second, my inside filled with light.

Her face lit up, and her eyes reflected my fire. She looked at me with such pure joy that my flame seemed to grow a little more, as if it wanted to embrace her.

"See?" said the man. "Now this one takes care of us too."

She smiled, satisfied, and rested her head on her father's shoulder. In that instant, I knew something inside me had changed. It wasn't just the warmth of the fire; it was something deeper, something new. I didn't know the word for it, but I understood it as affection.

From that night on, the girl came again. Not always, but often enough that I began to wait for her. Sometimes she came holding her father's hand; other times she ran ahead of him, laughing. Every time she saw me lit, she lifted her eyes with the same smile as the first night. She would stare at my light and say things that made me feel alive.

"Daddy, do lamp posts feel?" she would ask. "Because this one looks at me like it understands."

Her father laughed and told her lamp posts only shine, but she didn't seem convinced.

"I think this one gets sad when it rains," she said, "because the rain might put it out."

And though no one could hear me, she was right. The rain made me sad — not because of the water, but because it made me tremble, lose strength, and fear my light wouldn't be enough to accompany her.

One night, while her father talked with a friend, the girl came close to me. She looked at me tenderly and, without saying a word, took a ribbon from her hair. Carefully, she tied it around my base.

"Now you're not alone anymore," she whispered.

If I could have, I would have thanked her. From then on, the ribbon danced with me every night, moving with the wind as if it were my own memory of her.

The years passed, and the girl grew up. Her voice changed, her steps became longer, but her gaze still had the same light. Every time my spark was lit — even if it was her father who held the lamp — I knew the fire was born from her.

I don't know when she stopped coming. But I still keep her ribbon. And every night, when the wind moves it, I feel that she returns a little, that her laughter once again slips between the park's leaves, and that my light, for a few seconds, becomes the one from that first day.

Chapter Two – The Loneliness of Light

Time passes differently for me. I have no way to count the years, only the nights. Each spark that is born inside me is a new life, and each dawn, a farewell. I have seen how the leaves change color, how the benches wear down, how the paths fill and empty with faces that never return. But nothing hurt as much as the first time she stopped coming.

At first, I thought she had only been delayed. Every night I waited to see her figure approaching, to hear her voice speaking with her father, or the sound of a book opening beneath my light. But the days passed, and only the man came — alone, with tired steps. He no longer held anyone's hand. He lit my wick in silence and continued on his way without a word.

The park was still the same, but I was not. My light carried a sadness I could not hide. I felt the emptiness of her absence, as if I had been extinguished from within, even while still burning. The ribbon she had left me remained tied to my base. The wind moved it every night, and watching it dance was the only thing that reminded me she had been real.

One summer evening, some children came running. They played by throwing stones from one side of the path to the other. They laughed loudly, without thinking about what was around them. One of those stones hit my glass. The blow made me tremble. I heard the sound of the crystal cracking, and I felt how a small part of me broke away. It was a piece of my eye — the one that protected my flame. It did not break completely, but the crack let the wind in and made me burn with pain.

More nights passed, and the same children returned. This time they did not bring stones but curiosity. They saw the old, faded ribbon the girl had tied around me and began to pull at it. They tried to tear it off, pulling from side to side. The knot was tight, hardened by years and rust. The fabric frayed but did not give way. After several attempts, a stronger boy pulled with both hands, and the knot came loose. The ribbon fell to the ground, dirty and torn. They laughed a little and ran away. I kept looking at the piece of fabric until the wind carried it off.

That night, when the man came to extinguish me, I no longer wanted to wake again. My glass was cracked, my body rusted, and I no longer had her ribbon. I felt empty, old, useless. For the first time in all my years, I did not wish for the next night to arrive. I thought perhaps it was time to let the darkness do its work and allow myself to sleep forever.

But fate had other plans. When the sun fell once more, I heard the man's footsteps approaching. He lit my flame, as always, calmly and without saying a word. The spark grew again inside me, though this time it did so heavily. My light came out trembling, tired, but still alive. And then I saw her. It was her. She was no longer a little girl. She was a woman now, with the same eyes, the same gaze that had once been reflected in my fire. She walked slowly, stopped in front of me, and looked at me for a long time. Her expression changed: first surprise, then sadness. She came closer, ran her hand along my rusted base, and touched the mark where the ribbon had been so many years ago.

"Poor thing..." she whispered softly. "You look so old now..."

Her eyes filled with tears. Then she did something I never imagined — she hugged me. She pressed her forehead against my cold metal and wrapped her arms around me. Her warmth was so real that I thought my fire rekindled because of her. I felt that all the pain, the years of waiting, and the empty nights suddenly made sense for that one instant.

"I'm sorry," she murmured. "I never came back... I didn't take care of you."

She smiled through her tears and looked up toward my light, which flickered on her face. For a moment, I thought all the world's sadness and tenderness were contained in her eyes. And then I understood: that feeling I had been trying to name since I existed — what she had taught me without knowing — was love. Not the love that asks or demands, but the kind that simply exists; the kind that is content to illuminate another's path, even when the other does not stay.

Chapter Three – The Last Night

For a few days, I felt alive again. She returned to the park several times, and each night she brought with her a piece of light that seemed stronger than my own. The first night she came back after so many years, she noticed the crack in my glass and looked at me sadly. Without a word, she took a small piece of fabric from her bag and placed it gently over the opening, fastening it so the wind would not enter.

"There, that's better," she said quietly. "I don't want you to go out because of the cold."

Then she looked down at my base and smiled when she saw the spot where her old ribbon had once been. Without hesitation, she untied a new ribbon from her hair and tied it there patiently, just as she had done when she was a child.

"There," she whispered. "Now you're whole again."

That night my flame burned brighter than ever. In the days that followed, she returned several times. She did not speak much, but her presence was enough. I liked watching her sit on the bench, as before, with a book resting on her knees. She no longer read aloud, but her lips moved, and I could imagine the words. Everything seemed to have found its place again. I, the lamp post on the path, once more had a reason to shine.

But joy, like all light, also has its time. One evening, the sky turned a strange red, as if it knew something was about to end. I saw the man — the same one as always — walking toward me again, but this time he was not alone. She walked beside him. They moved slowly, speaking in low voices. When they arrived, the man stopped in front of me and prepared his lamp to light me, but she stopped him with her hand.

"Let me do it, Father," she said.

He nodded and handed her the rod with the flame. She approached me carefully and lit my wick. The spark rose weakly at first, then caught strength. For a moment, everything was as it had been before: the brightness, her smile, the warmth. But this time, there was something different in her gaze — a serene sadness.

"Father," she said after a pause. "This will be the last time I come. I'm leaving for another country. My husband is waiting for me. I won't be coming back. I just wanted to say goodbye to this place... and to him."

She turned toward me. Her eyes filled with tears, but her smile stayed firm.

"Thank you," she whispered. "Thank you for taking care of me, for keeping my secrets, for waiting for me all these nights."

The man said nothing. He only watched as she stepped closer. She extended her hand and touched me, with the same delicacy of that little girl who once believed lamp posts could feel.

"Don't cry for me," she murmured. "Everything I was, you already hold in your light."

She pressed her forehead against my cold body for a second, then turned away. She walked slowly, without looking back. Her father followed a few steps behind, and together they disappeared among the trees.

The night went on, but for me it ended there. I felt the absence like a hollow in my soul — though I have no soul. My light trembled, and the wind blew harder, as if it wanted to keep me company in silence. I looked at the empty bench and knew this was my last complete night. The new ribbon still fluttered, and within it lingered her scent, her farewell, her memory.

When dawn came, the man returned to extinguish me, as he did every day. He stopped in front of me and looked for a moment, not understanding why my flame seemed so weak. He turned the key gently, and the light went out.

The next day, a new worker from the town came. He checked my base, lit the rod, but my spark did not respond. He tried several times, until he gave up. He made a note in his book and walked away. No one tried again.

I have no fire now, but I am not empty. Inside me lives something stronger than flame: the memory of having felt, of having been seen, of having had a purpose. I was a lamp post, but she taught me what it was to be human. And though night still falls over the park, though my body rusts and my glass shatters, somewhere within me still shines her voice, her laughter, her tenderness.

Perhaps I no longer light anyone's path, but I light what I once was. And that, for me, is enough.

End of Story

About the Author

Gretter Luis de la Moneda writes under the pen name G. L. Monette. Her work explores memory, identity and the emotional traces left by loss. Her stories focus on characters searching for light within silence, blending introspection with richly symbolic imagery. For her, writing is an act of healing and a way to connect with what is deeply human.

Adult Published Finalist

End of Summer
William Teets

The hay makes my nose itch. My eyes have water in them, too. Maybe it's all them horses or all the dry weather we havin'. Either way, I still ain't gettin' no closer. I don't even know why I'm lookin'. Don't even know why I'm here.

The only other time I'd seen one, I had bad nightmares. All I saw was the faces of hares and jackals caught in Uncle Bartholomew's angry metal clamps. That's what it reminds me of at the end. Eyes all bugged-out and tongues just lollin' in their own blood and spit. I should be home doin' chores, but like I said, it's a dry September. Weren't much growin' goin' on. Ain't gonna be much harvest. Seems like there never is.

Mama tries though. Day after day she's out there in our dyin' garden tryin' to save them sickly crops. And she does save some, but not enough. I worry about her, but ain't never let her know I do. Just would make things worse. Ruin the few good times we have, remind us we won't have much come Thanksgiving.

But I still love Thanksgiving. Even if it ain't always bountiful. Even if sometimes there ain't much to be thankful for. Papa Preach plays his fiddle and Daddy's like lightenin' strikin' when he picks his dobro. So fast. I fool around clangin' some bells I tied to a tree branch, and Lucky Blue blows a harp like Sonny Boy Williamson. And of course, you best believe we all dance. Put old Scratch himself to shame.

After all that ruckus, Grandma Tilly tells stories 'bout the olden days. 'Bout pickin' cotton on Colonel Stoneman's plantation, and how one time she even ran off some Bluebellies. Talks about the Colonel's big white house and all his fancy to-dos and gadgets for makin' life easy. His life, at least.

At the end of her storytelling, Grandma Tilly gets all serious and sorrowful. Talks low. Almost mean. Tells 'bout how her sister Sarah was sold down the river, and how that scoundrel Colonel Stoneman came-a-callin' at night. Says her Eli would've killed him for sure, but he was sold off, too. She ain't never seen either of them again. And then like a windstorm blowin' up out of the hollow, Grandma Tilly jumps to her feet and shouts for everyone to start singin' to the Lord. We all hoot and dance and carry on loud enough to raise the dead. Ghosts be damned, we forget anything bad.

White folks sure know how to have a big ole celebration, too. 'Specially on a day like this. The main street and village square be all filled up with people just like when a carnival comes to town. They even have a parade. All the booted-up men kick up dust from the dry street, and all the women in fancy dresses clap their hands and nod their smiled faces. Children in their Sunday best be stompin' they feet, too, and wavin' sparklers and tiny American flags given to them by drunk soldiers. And don't even ask me 'bout all the firecrackers and gun shots. Sounds like a war's goin' on.

Even though I shouldn't be where I am, knowin' nightmares are just awaitin' for me down the line, I'm a stay. The dry hay and horse smell ain't too bad, even though my nose and eyes still itch. My ears ain't got no problem, though, hearin' the clatter comin' up the street.

Bringing up the rear of the parade, is four men makin' a hell of a rumpus. One man has a drum strapped up on him that's bigger than his big ole belly. Every time he pounds on it, I swear to Mother Mary I feel the beat rattle the bones in my chest. A second white man's blowin' like Gabriel into a long trumpet, just a slidin' a piece of it back-and-forth. Another bangs on a real tambourine with what sounds like a thousand Christmas bells all a ringin' at once. Puts my bells on a stick to shame. The last man scrapes and clatters on a washboard, kickin' his feet out while he does. All that's why I don't hear the voice creep up like a church mouse behind me.

"What you doing, darkie?"

I damn near jump out my skin. Whirl around like a tornado ready to rassle or run, when I see the voice is from a little white boy no more than six or seven. I just look down to the ground and says, "Nothin."

"You best be movin' on then. I got to get going, myself," he says. "I want to be up front when it starts."

I just keep silent.

And off he goes. As quick and quiet as how he come. I don't know why, but my soul shivers watchin' that young'un. Like someone done walked over my grave. He strolls away, nary a worry in the world. I wonder if he has nightmares too, or sleeps like a babe in the woods, sleep like he's protected by angels.

The homemade marchin' band stops playin', and the whole square is quiet now. Like walkin' through a graveyard by yourself on Hallows Eve quiet. I sees a man spit a gob of tobacco juice onto the dry dusty street, and I swear I hear a thud as it hits the ground. The colors of the white folks' clothes, the horse smell and hay of the stable, everything around me gets louder, if that makes any sense. I tingle all over, but not in a good feelin' way.

Mayor Evermore waddles his sloppy self up the wooden stairs and talks to the people. Looks to me from where I stand, he's a bit soused. He harrumphs and points to the sky with one his hands, and pounds his fist on the podium in front of him with his other. Speckles of spit fly from his mouth. Looks like Preacher Goodman-Brown does sometimes when he gives a Sunday sermon. Folks all up-and-down their heads and a few shout, "That's right, Mayor. Not here. Not ever."

I get lost in myself as his words fade away from me. Wonder again why I'm here. Welcoming ghosts that are surely gonna haunt me later. Maybe haunt me forever. I reaffirms with myself that in two more years, when I turn sixteen, I'm gone. Gone north to Chi-Town or Detroit or Pittsburgh. Leave all this sickness of spirit, Jim Crow hisself, far behind. Get a job in one of them factories assemblin' things. Dance with Can-Can girls on Saturday night, while bluesmen sing sweet sad songs of home.

A loud sneer and hoof thuds from snortin' horses, along with the blast of a twelve-gauge, scares me back to my senses quicker than a fox jumpin' through a forest fire. I see four hooded horsemen high-steppin their steeds through the crowd like Moses partin' the Red Sea. Buford Apple's boy, Samuel, is bein' led behind them, feet and hands bound, dirty rag stuck in his mouth. He's all bloody and busted up.

I'm not sure if words can be given a meanin' by just a look, but the look in Samuel's eyes is the most proper way to describe the word fear. And ugly, ugly is the look on all these white folks' faces. They cat-calling and scrunching their brows and snarling their teeth. Spewing forth curses and ills they'd beat their children for just thinking of. Feels like someone else, hell, a bunch of someone else's, stampeded over my grave.

Samuel is dragged up them same stairs Mayor Evermore walked just prior. He's led to the same spot the podium was at just a minute before. The white folks are in frenzy. Stone-cold mad. Jabbing at the air like they's punchin', strikin' poor Samuel. I don't see him, but I know the Fallen One is nearby just a hidin' in the bushes and clappin' his hands, too.

With a hush over the crowd, I can hear my own heartbeat. Squinch my eyes tight, hold all my air in my lungs. I hears that sickly thump, and a gasp, and then cheers and more gun shots fired into the heavens.

The bottom has fallen out.

Through all the noise, wafting-blue gun smoke, curses, denouncements, and sparklers burning out the crowd, the women and children start headin' back to whence they came. Men are corralling into the local gin mill, slappin' backs, and grinnin' ear to ear.

I leave the manger.

Walk toward the gallows against my better judgement.

Stand and stare at Samuel hung limp from a noose, neck broken. Just like the one time before that I saw. Samuel's eyes bulge too, his tongue lolled and swolled. Just like Uncle Bartholomew's critters caught in his metal jaws of death. Just like the hares and jackals in my nightmares.

I want Samuel to awake, or at least give me a sign he's at peace. Maybe to grant peace to me. To quiet the storm that's thunderin' in my head. Seein' him hung here enrages me, but oddly 'nough, seein' him is making me stronger somehow, too, almost at a ease. I'm confused as to how I can harvest anything good from this abomination, but I am, in real weird way. Bunch of mixed-up feelings running through my blood.

I remember back on how I used to fish with Samuel, catch bullfrogs in the swamp. He was funny and a good friend. Sweet and righteous. Full of life. But that's all taken. Taken away too soon. They say he looked lasciviously at a white woman. They rode horses to his house in the middle of the night. They tore him from his mother's clutch, decided he needed to die. Samuel weren't but fifteen.

I run home fast. Like a hellhound is on my tail. All kinds of pictures fill up my mind as I race down Myers Corner, kickin' up dust from the dry road. My tears are wet and plenty, but they dry by the wind in my face just as quick as they come. I run past Saint Peter's Church where we pray, past Hillside Cemetery where we go when we die. I think again about how in two more years I'm gonna leave for the North. How maybe I'll tell stories, like Grandma Tilly does, to my grandchildren, about the olden days. Maybe during Thanksgiving. Stories and song and dance to celebrate them that came before. Stories of Samuel. All if I live that long, with hopefully happier times to come. I mean things ain't gonna stay like this forever. Right? Don't make no sense. Just can't be.

Then I picture, what if they come for me in the night? Come for me next time?

About the Author

William Teets born in Peekskill, NY, has recently relocated to Southeast Michigan. He misses New York pizza, the Hudson River and seeking sanctuary in favorite haunts, far from impulses of the gods. Mr. Teets' poetry and prose have been published in numerous literary journals and anthologies, including *Blood+Honey, Ariel Chart, Ink in Thirds* and *Impspired.* He is the author of two poetry books, *After the Fall* (2023) and

Babylon Redux (2025), both published by Cajun Mutt Press.

Adult Published Finalist

Present Tense
Jill Hinton Wolfe

The text came while Garrett was feeding the Herefords—six words that changed the temperature of the February air: Ortiz didn't make it. Funeral's Saturday.

He stood in the barn doorway, phone in his gloved hand, watching his breath crystallize. His dog, Bodhi, pressed against his leg thirty seconds before the smell hit—that sharp, metallic tang of gunfire that had no business being in Curtis, Michigan. Garrett counted the rafters. One, two, three.

Focused on the cold burning his lungs. Four, five, six. The phantom smell faded.

Bodhi stayed close as Garrett finished chores. The dog had been with him four months, three longer than Garrett had been home. A brindle pit mix with a blocky head and amber eyes that tracked every move—sixty-five pounds of muscle and awareness. People at the VA said Bodhi had washed out of explosives work: too sensitive, they said. He'd been retrained for a different kind of detection. A different kind of bomb.

Garrett's father was in the kitchen when he came in, stamping snow off his boots. The old man looked up from his paper.

"Everything squared away?"

"Yeah." Garrett peeled off his gloves. "Got a text. Ortiz died."

His father nodded once. Didn't ask who Ortiz was, didn't need to.

"Funeral?"

"Saturday. Downstate."

"You going?"

Garrett didn't know yet. He said he'd think about it.

Maya called while he was in the shower. He almost didn't answer, but Bodhi was staring at the phone like it might explode, so he did.

"Hey," she said. Her voice had that diner-shift rasp—eight hours of calling orders and refilling coffee. "Can I come by tomorrow? I get off at three."

"Yeah. Sure."

"You okay? You sound weird."

"I'm fine. Just tired."

She didn't believe him, but she let it go. That was Maya—patient until she wasn't.

That night, Bodhi slept pressed against his side, the way he always did. But Garrett couldn't sleep. Every time he closed his eyes he was back there: the weight of his rifle, the taste of dust, Harmon making jokes about his ex-wife, Ortiz humming an old Mariachi tune while he cleaned his M4.

Around three a.m. Garrett gave up and went to the window. The Upper Peninsula stars were brutal in their clarity. He wondered if Ortiz had looked up at stars in Flint before he injected whatever it was that stopped his heart.

The night seemed alive with threads, crossing and tightening—past, present, and something not yet. The lines wavered: Garrett in the barn, Garrett in the Humvee, Garrett at a funeral that hadn't happened yet. Somewhere in the dark, Bodhi gave a low whine. Something in the weave had shifted.

Morning came gray and heavy with snow. Garrett woke already dressed in his old USMC PT pants. He didn't remember getting out of bed or pulling them on.

The coffee pot was still warm. Bodhi watched him with unusual intensity as Garrett poured a cup and watched the steam rise, steady as breath. His hands needed something to hold.

His father was already out on a plow run—some county road near Manistique. A note on the table read: Back by dinner. Coffee's on.

Maya showed up at three-fifteen, still in her work clothes. Her nametag said MAYA in block letters above a coffee stain. She smelled like maple syrup and exhaustion.

She'd waited for him—four years, two deployments—and Garrett still couldn't figure out why.

They sat at the kitchen table. She talked about spring—maybe they could drive up to Marquette when the weather broke, maybe take the ferry to Grand Island. Garrett's eyes kept drifting to the silver ring on her left hand, the cheap one he'd bought at a tourist shop before shipping out.

His own hands still wouldn't stop trembling.

Bodhi moved between them, creating space. Maya noticed.

"You're disappearing again," she said.

"I'm right here."

"No." Her voice was soft but certain. "You're not."

She stood, set her mug in the sink. Garrett wanted to answer, but his throat had closed. The kitchen was too bright, the hum of the refrigerator too loud.

Maya kissed the top of his head. "Call me when you get back," she said, and left.

His father came home an hour later, read the room, and said only, "Road needs plowing. Long driveway's drifted shut."

He gave Garrett a task. Something to do with his body.

Garrett took the old F-250 with the blade mounted in front. Bodhi climbed into the passenger seat, vest on. He knew the difference between work and not-work.

Snow came down hard—that U.P. snow that erased the world, turned everything white and infinite. Garrett dropped the blade and pushed white into white.

The truck's heater rattled. The wipers scraped ice. Bodhi sat perfectly still, watching.

And then—

The whiteout became dust.

The truck became a Humvee.

Harmon was driving, telling a story about his cousin's graduation party. Ortiz in back, quietly staring out the bulletproof window. The smell of diesel and fear-sweat. The weight of Garrett's rifle across his knees.

Bodhi barked—sharp, urgent, wrong—but Garrett couldn't hear him over the ringing in his ears, over the—

The IED hit like God's fist.

The truck slammed into a snowbank. Stopped hard.

Time folded.

Two Garretts: one in the truck, breathing cold air; one in the Humvee, back in the heat and dust.

The world tilted between them, threads crossing and pulling tight. Bodhi barked again, as if trying to hold the two halves together.

For an instant, Curtis snow bled into Helmand dust.

Garrett was in both places at once.

The truck cab. The Humvee.

Michigan snow. Afghan sand.

And Bodhi was there too—impossible but real. A brindle dog in a war zone where there had been no dog.

The memory unfolded as it always did: Ortiz hurt bad, screaming. Harmon shouting into the radio.

Garrett had to choose—stay with Ortiz and try to stop the bleeding, or secure the perimeter, the way he'd been trained.

He chose the mission.

By the time CASEVAC arrived, Ortiz had stopped screaming.

Ortiz survived. Lived two more years. Got clean, got dirty, got clean again. Now dead, last week, needle in a motel bathroom off I-75.

But here—in this layered place where past and present touched— Garrett saw something he hadn't before:

Ortiz didn't die because Garrett chose wrong.

His thread just frayed faster. The blast had burned through more than flesh—it scorched the part that held him here.

Garrett had been carrying both ends ever since, mistaking one thread for the other.

The air shimmered around him, trembling like heat. It held him there— between then and now—until he understood: he could visit the past without drowning in it.

Retrieve what he needed. Then come back.

Garrett reached for the version of Ortiz who was still breathing, still humming under his breath, still alive. He didn't try to change the ending. He only said, "I'm sorry."

To Ortiz. To Harmon. To himself.

The Humvee dissolved. Snow rushed in. Diesel became winter air.

He was back in the truck, the front end crumpled into a drift, steam curling from the grille.

Bodhi beside him, trembling but steady.

Garrett looked down. The dog's muzzle was grayer now. Along his spine, seven white hairs—new ones—stood out against the brindle.

"I'm sorry," Garrett whispered again, this time to the dog.

Bodhi's tail thumped once.

By the time he reached the house, his father was waiting at the door.

He didn't ask what happened to the truck. Just helped Garrett inside, made more coffee, sat with him at the kitchen table.

Garrett told him about Ortiz. About the choice. About the funeral on Saturday.

"You going?" his father asked again.

"Yeah," Garrett said. "I have to."

He texted Maya: I'm sorry. Can we talk?

She answered right away: Yes.

That night, Bodhi curled against him. Garrett ran his hand along the dog's spine, counting the white hairs again. Seven. One for each time Bodhi had pulled him back—or followed him in.

"We're keeping score now?" he murmured.

Bodhi sighed, already half asleep.

Saturday morning, Garrett put on his dress blues. The uniform still fit, almost. The mirror showed a man leaner than before, worn smooth by time.

Bodhi wore his service vest, red nylon with the globe and anchor, SERVICE DOG stitched in white.

The drive south took three hours through snow and pine. The funeral was in Grand Rapids, at the veteran's cemetery, rows of white headstones like teeth.

Marines he half remembered stood in clusters, talking in low voices.

When the bugler played taps, Garrett stood at attention, Bodhi steady at his left side.

After the flag was folded, he knelt by the casket. Laid a hand on the polished wood. Bodhi leaned against him—solid, warm, alive. Present moment. Present life.

The air was sharp enough to hurt. Garrett welcomed the sting.

They drove home in silence. When the highway narrowed to two lanes, he called Maya. She answered on the first ring.

"Hey," he said.

"Hey." He could hear her smile.

"Tomorrow okay? I need to help my dad with some plow runs."

"Tomorrow's perfect."

That night, Garrett sat on the porch. The stars were the kind that belonged to the U.P.—merciless, clear, endless. Inside, his father's TV murmured through the walls. Tomorrow there would be roads to clear, dogs to feed, a woman waiting to talk.

Bodhi rested beside him, wrapped in an old blanket. His head on Garrett's knee, breath slow and even. Another white hair had appeared—an eighth thread in the weave.

Garrett touched it lightly.

"The thread held," he whispered.

Bodhi's tail thumped once.

Present. Present. Present.

About the Author

Jill Hinton Wolfe is a Michigan-based writer and U.S. Army veteran. Her fiction leans quiet and slightly uncanny, with a focus on memory, place and what lingers. She writes about people learning how to stay present while carrying what came before. Jill navigates the world with her guide dog, Hannah, who has strong opinions about squirrels and pacing.

Adult Published Finalist

Student of Dreams
Joy VerHoef

My phone rang as I walked back from class. The heart-wrenching lyrics of Rick Astley's one-hit wonder poured from my pocket. Two of my lab mates, River and Liam, began sniggering behind me. Emmi, the unofficial mom of the group, immediately turned and glared at the boys. "You did not Rickroll Michelle's phone!"

Their only response was an explosion of loud laughter. Laughing myself, I turned to Emmi and murmured, "Don't worry, I've already set up a surprise for them. Just make sure that they boot up the lab PC on Thursday."

As she smiled and nodded in response, a frisbee careened toward her from the green space outside the dorm. Not missing a beat, she caught it. Despite the chill of late fall, there always seemed to be students playing frisbee. Shivering and pulling my hood up to cover my dark brown hair, I thought longingly of the warm humidity of my home. The weak rays of light, struggling through the empty tree branches seemed a poor substitute for the strength of the Ecuadorian sun.

"Wanna give frisbee another shot, Shorty?" River called to me as he ran to get open for Emmi.

"No, I think that call was from my aunt. I should call her back." I said, grateful for any excuse to escape standing outside in the cold a moment longer than necessary. "One of my cousins probably lost a tooth or something super important like that."

Shrugging, River jumped to catch the disc intentionally thrown high by Emmi. "You do you." He said as he and Liam ran off to join the small group of kids calling for the return of their frisbee.

Emmi called after them, "See you tomorrow to put together that report. Remember, I'm bringing donuts!"

I chuckled softly; she seemed convinced that no one would show up without food. Glancing back at Liam and River, I smiled. She was probably right.

After Emmi and I walked the final few steps into the dorm, I pulled off my faux fur lined hood. My coat had been my largest purchase upon arriving in the States. Calling to me from the clearance rack, it offered a reminder of the warmth of home in its navy folds. The purchase hadn't left me much spending money, but I knew I could make up the loss with an internship. I just had to work hard enough so a company would be willing to pay to sponsor a work visa.

As I turned to climb the stairs to my room, Emmi said, "My roommate and I are watching Parks and Rec reruns after she gets out of work tonight. Wanna join?"

Before I could answer, my phone rang again, causing a group of students walking in behind us to stare; one even started to dance. "Maybe," I laughed. "I should really take this call."

A smile still playing at the corners of my mouth, I anticipated the excited bubble of chatter that thinly linked me to my family. Lifting my phone, I said, "Hola, Tía!" I was answered by a sob.

"Tía?" I began climbing the stairs faster, hoping to get someplace private. "What's wrong? What's going on?"

Her words jumbled together with tears and entreaties to God. She repeated my name. She repeated my papi's name. I forced my key into the dorm room lock and opened the door to a thankfully dark room. My roommate was out.

A thin ray of light streamed through the partially closed blinds, casting a line across the floor to my side of the room. I threw my backpack and coat onto the chair and settled onto my bed.

"Tía, I can't understand you." My voice shook, fear climbing up from my stomach and drawing tight every muscle on its march to my head.

She drew a deep breath and managed, "It's your papi, mi ángel. They've taken him."

"Who?" My breathing sped up. Dread settled into my gut. I knew the answer.

"They said that we must have a lot of money. You are studying at a big university in the United States. They said that everyone who lives in the United States is rich." She broke down into sobs again.

"Who?" I almost wailed. "Who said? Who has Papi?"

"Los Tiguerones." Her voice was lost again in sobs and prayers.

Darkness. Everything was dark and frozen. No, not the gang, my mind pleaded. Tía continued weeping and speaking. I could not hear her. A continuous ringing silence filled my ears.

"You must send us money!" Snapping back, I heard her plea. "You must send us whatever you have! They have given us twenty-four hours. We can still save him."

"Tía, I don't have any money." My voice was quiet, filled with misery. I was too slow. I should have worked harder, gotten into school sooner. Then maybe I could have protected my family. "My tuition, my room, my food, my books, even my flight, they were all covered by the scholarship. I don't even have enough money to buy a bag of chips."

"Then you must sell whatever you can." She was my old tía again, commanding and firm. "Anything, everything. You must sell it now and send us the money. We have until 3p.m. tomorrow night to get enough. Do not talk to the American police. If they contact the gang, they will ask for more money. They will say that we are very well connected. They will kill your father in some terrible, public way to get the news to report on it."

I slowly deflated from a confident engineering student into a tiny sliver of a human. "Ok, Tía. I'll try," I said as we ended the call.

I gazed around at the entirety of my possessions: pens, pictures, notebooks – nothing anyone would buy. My eyes drifted over to my chair. My coat, my precious coat, it was beautiful and warm and full of dreams. Maybe it would be worth more now that it was colder and closer to winter?

Pulling open my backpack, I drew out my textbooks and my laptop. Both had been given to me as part of my scholarship. My laptop hadn't been new, just recycled from a past student, yet it was the key to my dream future. But what would my future be without Papi? I could use the lab computers for my assignments. I didn't need a laptop. Surely, someone would still buy it.

I didn't have much, but my papi had many friends and my tía was a force to be reckoned with. We could get enough money. I would sell what I could, contribute how I could and it would be ok.

Not willing to lose any time, I transferred all of my files to my student cloud account and wiped my PC. After, cleaning it up the best I could, I set off for the IT department. They bought old computers for technology students to break and fix.

I was a little worried. I hadn't actually bought the computer; it was part of my scholarship. But they had given it to me. It was mine, then, right? I could sell it if I wanted.

The guy at the IT desk called his manager. A distracted man in his late fifties emerged. Glancing briefly at me over the top of the machine as he inspected it, he asked, "What's wrong with it? Why are you selling?"

I wiped my sweating palms on my coat and replied hesitantly, "I, um, don't need it anymore."

An incessant beeping noise began in the back room. Swearing, the manager turned to the student running the desk, "Transfer her the standard $50 for a working laptop." Then he stomped angrily into the back room.

Relieved, I walked away. If I wasn't allowed to sell it, surely, he would have refused to buy it. After all, he was a manager.

#

The next morning, I walked to the bank and wired the collected money to my aunt. Shivering, I wrapped my arms around myself. My coat, my most beloved and expensive purchase in this frozen wasteland of a city, was now being hung up in the front of a consignment shop by a man who knew all too well that he had underpaid me for it.

My thoughts warred with each other. Hope declared, I tried my best and pulled together what I could. Everything is going to be alright. Reason responded, It's not enough. I should have worked harder at finding a job when I got here. It's not enough.

Numb both inside and out, I walked back to campus. Mists of thought swirled through my mind, sometimes broken by a glimpse of hope, sometimes obscuring everything in the depth of despair.

Out of the fog, Emmi appeared. "Hey, we've been waiting for you for like an hour! Where have you been? And please don't be too angry" – dramatic pause – "River ate your donut." She threw her hands up defensively. "I couldn't stop him!"

I paused and turned toward her, blinking in a desperate attempt to connect the theme of donuts to the shadows churning within me. "So...?" she asked. "Did you finish your portion of the report?" Then gasping theatrically and emphasizing each word she almost yelled, "Where is your coat? I have never seen you take that thing off. I thought it was fused to your body."

"I'm sorry." I heard myself mumble. "I'm not feeling well. I think I need to go to my room. I'll email my portion tonight."

"I'll bet you're not feeling well!" She exclaimed as I walked away. "Go put your coat on."

The rest of the day passed, both too long and too short. My tía called me throughout the day with updates. My family sold what they could and begged from everyone. Most of our friends had nothing to give but sympathy. We were not the first to lose a member of our family to the gangs.

Oddly enough, my heart refused to stop hoping. Every time I answered the phone, it was with the expectation that I would hear my papi's voice. He would tell me that everything was ok and he would lecture me about wasting my time worrying about him when I should have been studying. Despite the increasing despair seeping through my tía's voice, my heart reached for the light.

I sat in near darkness when the call came from Tía at 10:30. They had been sent a video showing the execution of my father. The last flicker of hope inside me died, and, strangely, a flash of relief traveled through my body. There was no more uncertainty. My father's life was over. There was nothing I could do.

Throughout the night, anger, helplessness, regret, sadness, and self-recrimination danced a complicated rhythm inside my body and mind, crescendoing into an overwhelming flood before spiraling down into emptiness. A single thought was enough to restart the sickening dance. I found no peace that night and I didn't seek it. How could there be peace or hope again?

My alarm rang at 6 in the morning. Hazily, I began to get ready for the day, a flicker of determination, unwilling to be completely quenched, began to grow in my mind. I could not save my papi, but if I worked hard, I could still help my family. I had to. I had to be better than before. I had to work harder than before. I would not fail again.

A knock sounded on my door. Confused, I opened it to see my RA and two members of the campus police. My heart rate picked up, my thoughts beginning their frenetic dance. Oh no. Something else. It's not going to be ok. It's never going to be ok.

One of them spoke, "If you would come with us, Miss Andrade, we have a few questions that we need to ask you regarding your laptop."

Swaying slightly, I followed them. I couldn't remember the last time I had eaten. Had it only been a day? It felt like a million years separated me from the girl who had traded pranks with her friends.

We were silent as we walked the quiet paths to the campus security building. Since class had just started, there weren't many people out, just those running late. I saw Liam slip in the mathematics building. I vaguely wondered who he would sit by since I wasn't in class today to save him a seat.

It was snowing by the time we reached the building Big, lazy flakes drifted down sticking to my T-shirt. As we walked into the warm front office, they melted, dripping through my hair and leaving spots on my clothes.

I sat in a small office. The two officers sat across from me on the other side of the desk. One introduced himself and recited something that sounded like a memorized script before getting to the point. He pulled out my laptop and asked, "Did you sell this on Tuesday afternoon at approximately 5p.m.?"

Looking at my laptop, I felt tears start to form. I could still see the smudge where I'd tried to scrub off the sticky residue of my "Karma is Cat" sticker. That machine had been both my closest friend and my fiercest enemy as I'd wrestled with the complexities of computer language.

Without taking my eyes from the laptop, I nodded.

"Were you aware that this laptop was leased to you and it not actually your property?"

I shook my head.

Sighing, the office asked, "Can you tell me why you sold it?"

My voice began to speak; relaying all that had happened to me in the last forty-eight hours. Tears ran silently down my face, yet my voice continued, steady and calm. When I reached the part of the story in which my papi was killed, my voice faded to nothing.

The officers thanked me. Time passed. They gave me water. I heard the voice of the superintendent outside. "Excuse me, Mr. Senator, but you're not even a representative of Michigan. This really isn't your place to speak. Please wait outside."

An angry male voice responded, "Not my place? My place is wherever truth needs to outshine the lies of this stronghold of deception. This girl," I heard him move. "is a threat to all Americans and what America stands for. She has abused her student visa, selling borrowed property and then giving it to a terrorist organization. A visa is not a right; it is a privilege. This girl does not deserve that privilege. She is propagating violence and crime."

"With all due respect sir," the voice of the superintendent faded as they walked away, leaving me alone with the ringing in my ears.

Sometime later, the same officer returned and told me that I would have to move to another building. His voice sounded clouded and distant. I noticed him staring at me, expectantly. I had missed something. "Sorry, what did you say?" I heard my voice ask.

"Your coat," He said. "It's snowing really hard outside. Where's your coat?"

"I sold it." said my voice simply.

He looked at me for a few seconds before reaching behind the door and drawing out a beat up Carhartt jacket. He took some things from the pockets and threw them onto the desk before holding the coat out to me. "Would you like to use this one? It's too cold for anyone to be out there without one." Gesturing toward the door and the muffled sounds of an argument, he added, "We're not all like that."

I blinked in surprise. "Thank you," a small bud of hope began to bloom. Glancing down at the sturdy weave, I felt awkward. I would never buy something this utilitarian and it was weird to wear someone else's coat. I didn't even know this guy. But maybe, accepting help from strangers was the only way forward. I could almost see small threads of goodwill peeking through the coat's fibers. Maybe this wasn't the end of everything.

As we walked out the door, I saw Emmi waiting outside. "I'm sorry." I said as I was escorted to the waiting car. "I won't be able to finish my report."

Emmi walked alongside us. "Your report!" She was angry. "Your report! Is that seriously what you're worried about!" I sat down in the car. "I heard a bunch of nerf herders were going to kick you out of school, out of the country. They're saying crazy things about you. What the–" Her words were cut off by the closing of the door.

#

There were lawyers, police, angry protestors, embassy staff, politicians, friends, and passing days all culminating with today. Right now. I stared out my window as the airplane slowly taxied into its bay. Numbly, I stood, wrapped my coat tightly around me, and walked off the plane.

My feet carried me through customs, down endless hallways, and to the baggage claim. I wandered toward the door; my tía had promised to meet me and join for the taxi ride home. As I stepped outside, I was greeted by a warm hug of hot, humid air. Slipping off my stifling coat-it's threads now empty of dreams-I welcomed the embrace of my home.

My phone rang, the earnest voice of Rick Astley blending with the distant echo of gunshots. Never gonna let you down. Never gonna give you up. Glancing down at the caller id, I answered, "Hola Tía."

About the Author

Joy VerHoef is a software engineer who lives in Grandville, MI. She enjoys learning, walking and board games. This is a fictional story based off of various events that occurred during 2024-2025 and Joy's own experience living abroad.

Teen Judges' Choice Winner

Before I Forget
Charlize Sitto

I am the smartest person in my class. That is not boastfulness. That is arithmetic. That is observation, deduction, and empirical verification. I know the trajectory of thought, the subtle biases inherent in adolescent reasoning, the concatenation of error in the human intellect. I am acutely aware, in ways most people cannot begin to parse, that the mind is a network of nodes, firing in tandem and yet always self-referencing, collapsing upon itself in infinite regress if improperly stimulated. The visitors arrive. They always arrive in the most banal, efficient manner: three men in matching suits, crisp white shirts, polished shoes that click too loudly on the scuffed linoleum. They smile at the students with just enough warmth to seem human but not enough to seem fallible. Behind them, a projector whirs to life, displaying a hologram of a brain rotating slowly, glowing like a small, artificial sun.

"Your intelligence," intones the tallest man, whose tie is unnervingly straight, "is a resource. Why hoard it? Why allow it to stagnate in the vessels of inaction? Cognify offers a method to redistribute cognitive surplus. Exchange your potential for immediate, tangible benefits."

The auditorium is silent except for the faint buzzing of fluorescent lights.

I raise my hand, of course. It is instinctual.

"Excuse me," I say. "Are you claiming that intelligence is quantifiable, divisible, and transferable without loss or corruption?"

They do not flinch. The man with the unnerving tie smiles. "Precisely. We maintain rigorous protocols. The process is safe, scientifically validated, and ethical. Those who choose to participate are compensated handsomely for contributions that society deems surplus."

I glance around the room. My classmates are wide eyed. Some are skeptical; some are already scribbling down numbers, dreaming of paychecks or game consoles or attention.

I cannot reconcile my own amusement with my horror. I know, with a clarity that strikes me almost physically, that intelligence is not a currency. It is not divisible. It is not a thing that can be lent or borrowed without consequence. And yet, the promise of wealth and approval hovers in the air, tempting the poorly informed and the unreflective.

I leave the auditorium with Rachel, my closest peer in the class, though "peer" is a loose designation. She laughs easily, the kind of laugh that is contagious and warm, and she looks at me as though I am imagining complications that do not exist.

"You're overthinking it," she says. "Look, they give you money. That's it."

I laugh quietly, but the sound is dry, brittle. She does not notice the subtle tremor in my jaw. She doesn't notice a lot.

That night, I study. I create a schematic of the procedure on my bedroom floor, lining up variables like soldiers: expected cognitive output, loss ratios, potential compensation, ethical trade-offs, and systemic social impact. The numbers are elegant. I can map every possible permutation. Theoretically, there is no reason a human mind should suffer from a carefully measured contribution. Theoretically.

I also write an essay, as I always do, compiling references from neuroscience, moral philosophy, and economic theory. I submit it to my English teacher, who reads it with a combination of awe and terror. "Seraphine," she says, "you are terrifyingly brilliant."

I do not correct her.

A week later, I am called to the administration office for the first "consultation." They ask how much I am willing to offer. I say, cautiously, five points– a number derived from my own meticulous calculations, small enough to minimize risk yet sufficient to earn a meaningful reward.

The procedure is clinical, simple, almost mundane. A device rests against my temple. A quiet hum, a cold pressure, a slight tingling. I am instructed to remain still, to breathe, to think of nothing. I comply. It is easy to comply.

When it ends, I feel nothing. Absolutely nothing.

The technician hands me a card with my new cognitive index. One hundred seventy-nine. I calculate the difference from my previous score. The math is satisfying. I am compensated ten thousand credits, which is enough to pay tuition and rent for the year.

I walk home in the gray afternoon, carrying the weight of numbers and notes and potential. My thoughts feel lighter, not diminished but displaced, like books temporarily removed from a library shelf. I am delighted by the efficiency, by the clinical perfection of the transaction, by the absolute predictability of the outcome.

School continues. I notice that my classmates now speak to me differently, with more attention, more respect. My words are fewer, my sentences shorter. I shrug it off. Perhaps I am growing more direct. Perhaps the complexity of my speech was previously an impediment to social cohesion.

Rachel asks me about the procedure. "Did it hurt?" she says.

"No," I say. "It is inconsequential."

Weeks pass. I make another contribution. Twenty points this time, for a more lucrative reward.

It is comforting to feel that I am doing good, that my contributions serve a higher social function. By the third transfer, I am increasingly aware of lapses in memory. Minor equations evade me. Historical dates slip past recognition. I misplace notes. The teachers do not seem concerned. They praise my "clear, readable" work. My classmates nod approvingly when I speak in the cafeteria. I feel warmth. Approval.

One night, I stumble upon an old essay in my desk. I attempt to read it aloud. Words stumble. The intricate argument I once wove collapses into fragments. I laugh. "Too complicated," I murmur to myself. "Nobody needs that much thinking anyway."

The world seems sharper, brighter, more entertaining. Colors are vivid, food tastes sweeter, music is more immediate. The school feels less like a cage of intellect and more like a playground of sensation.

Dr. Lumen smiles at me during a routine check-in. "You are progressing nicely, Seraphine. Happiness and intelligence do not need to be correlated. You are learning that."

I nod. He has not lied. The sensation is real. Happiness is real. I even start to forget the specifics of my previous brilliance.

Another year passes. My contributions increase 50 points, 75 points. Each time, the procedures are smoother, more routine. My thinking becomes less precise, less meticulous. I cannot parse complex arguments. References fade. The intricate mental lattices I once constructed collapse into simple scaffolds. I smile. I am praised. People say I am radiant.

I do not notice that my laughter is easier to provoke, that my arguments are thin, that my attention span has shortened. I am content. I am social. I am agreeable.

The elite- those who purchase intelligence — watch me. They smile. They say I am exemplary. I nod. I cannot fathom why, but the feeling is warm and satisfying.

Two years later, I walk into the auditorium for the final procedure offered to me. One hundred points, nearly my entire surplus. I hesitate. I feel a faint unease. A shadow of curiosity, a flicker of the old self. But it passes. Dr. Lumen's smile is constant. He assures me: "You will be happier."

The procedure begins. I close my eyes. The hum envelops me. The cold pressure settles against my temples. I drift.

When I open my eyes, the world is simpler, friendlier, more forgiving. I do not remember what I lost, nor do I care. I see classmates. Friends. People smiling. I am included. I am loved. I am radiant.

I reflect occasionally, as I always have, but the reflection is shallow. Complex questions fade before reaching consciousness. Ethics, philosophy, morality- they are words without weight. I accept things. I am content. I am obedient. I am happy.

Sometimes I find old notebooks. They look foreign. I do not read them. I do not need to. Happiness is straightforward, uncomplicated. I have no concern for what has passed, only for the warmth of immediate approval, the simplicity of unchallenged joy.

Dr. Lumen watches from the sidelines. He is satisfied. The Bureau is satisfied. I am satisfied.

And yet, if I think- briefly, fleetingly- I feel something distant, something unnameable. A faint echo of the self I once was. I cannot grasp it. It fades. Happiness has replaced curiosity, simplicity has replaced wonder, contentment has replaced questioning.

I am happy.

The world applauds. I smile.

Morning light hums. It really hums now, or maybe that's the walls. I wake up to the slogan playing from the street below—

"A Brighter Mind Makes a Brighter World!"

The words used to sound ironic to me. I remember that—irony. That's the word, right? Means something like opposit… opposate. But now it just sounds nice. Warm.

I work at the Center now. The Bureau calls us Contributors. The posters on the walls are yellow, full of happy faces. "Give What You Don't Need," they say, in happy font that almost bounces. Sometimes the letters shimmer, like they're laughing. Maybe they are.

My job is easy. I file the reports of others who come in to make transfers. I sit at a little white desk, and a little white screen tells me who is next. I push the buttons that tell the machine they've come, and then they go behind the blue door where Dr. Lumen waits. (He doesn't look older, even though it's been… I forget. Time is slower here. Or faster. It's fine.)

At lunch we get nutrient bars that taste like vanilla and chalk. Everyone eats together and smiles a lot. We talk about how lucky we are. We all say it in the same tone, like reciting prayer. "We are lucky. We are bright. We are helpful."

It makes my chest warm to say it. The warmth is proof. Warmth means truth.

Sometimes new people come from the schools. Smart ones, like I was. They talk too fast, use big words. I like hearing them, but it hurts a bit too. Makes my head feel stretched, like chewing gum. One girl yesterday said "cognitive capitalism," and I laughed because that's such a funny sound. Cognicap.

She didn't laugh. She looked scared. Dr. Lumen took her aside. Later I saw her smiling, so it must've gone good.

They pay us every week. Credits. Numbers on screens that turn into food and shows and lights. We all buy the same shows–bright colors, jokes about cats that fall down stairs. Everyone laughs. I laugh too. It's good to be the same.

Sometimes, when the speakers hum between announcements, I think I hear whispers behind them.

"Don't waste the light."

"Don't think so much."

I tell myself it's just the vents. But the vents sound a lot like my old voice. The one that used to ask too many things. I think she's jealous. She can't understand how good it feels to stop asking.

The Bureau started a new thing—smaller transfers, more frequent. Keeps us "stable," they say. I don't really need the money but I like the chair and the way the machine hums. It's like sleeping, only cleaner. Afterward, the world looks smooth. Round. Easier to touch. Sometimes I forget things, like names of colors or people I used to know, but then Dr. Lumen smiles and says, "Memory is clutter."

And that sounds right. Clutter is bad.

Today a man came to the counter. He wore the gray badge. That means he buys thought. He had smooth hair and nice shoes, and his eyes were shiny, like polished coins.

"Efficient work you're doing here," he said. "We're all grateful for your contributions."

His words felt like honey poured in my ears. Sweet, heavy.

I smiled too big and said, "Thank you for buying."

He laughed but not in the friendly way. "Buying?" he said. "No, dear. We manage intelligence. We ensure balance."

Balance. That's a pretty word. Means equal. Means everyone happy. I like happy.

Still, something in his eyes—it flickered. Like he was holding laughter inside, laughter at me maybe. But it's fine. He's rich. They always smile funny. Their teeth are so white they glow.

At home my apartment is small but neat. Neat is good. The city outside hums like bees. On every corner are screens showing bright faces saying things like, "Thank you for sharing your mind!"

Sometimes the faces look like mine. Or maybe they are mine. I forget what I look like exactly. My mirror shows a girl with hair too thin and eyes that twitch when she tries to focus.

I write in my journal sometimes, like right now. It helps me practice words. Some are tricky now. Like "ph... phil..." something about thinking. Philophacy? I don't remember what it means but I think I used to like it. I don't like it now. It makes my head ache.

They've started calling for volunteers to permanent alignment. Sounds good. "Permanent" Dr. Lumen says permanent means forever. "Alignment" means right.

Everyone at lunch is excited. "We won't have to worry about choices anymore," says June. She has pretty hair and always remembers to smile the Bureau way—lips tight, eyes blank. I like her. She says I should do it too. Dr. Lumen says I'd be a perfect candidate. That word—perfect—makes my chest glow.

But sometimes, at night, I hear a tapping in the walls. Or maybe it's in my head. Tap tap tap. Like someone's trying to tell me a thing. Last night the tapping made words. "Don't," it said.

Don't what? I asked the dark, but the dark just hummed louder.

A new friend started today. His name is—or was—Evan. He sits at the desk next to mine. He's quiet but his eyes move fast. I like watching them. They move like I used to think.

He doesn't smile much. He asked me, "Seraphine, do you remember the theorem about diminishing returns?"

I laughed. "No, but it sounds funny! Diminish sounds like dinner."

He didn't laugh. He looked sad. Then he whispered, "They're taking everything. They're hollowing us."

I told him he shouldn't say weird things like that. The walls hear. He said he knows. He said the walls are made of us.

That's silly. But later, when I touched the wall, it felt soft, like skin.

Sometimes I forget where I work. Sometimes I forget the word for forget. But it's okay. The announcements always remind me. "Work is joy. Joy is clarity." They rhyme. Rhymes make truth.

Evan keeps whispering strange stuff. He says the Receivers never take the pills, never sit in the chairs. "If it's so good," he said today, "why don't they give too?"

I told him they don't need to. They're already happy. The Bureau says they manage overflow. He said, "No, they're stealing the light."

I laughed because stealing is bad and Dr. Lumen says nothing bad exists anymore.

But later, I thought maybe he meant something. Something I can't shape. It sits at the back of my skull, knocking. I try not to hear.

Evan stopped coming last week. They said he volunteered for full alignment. The morning after, his desk was gone. I asked Dr. Lumen if he was happy now. He said, "Extremely." Then he smiled that same big smile that never moves his eyes.

I think about volunteering too. The world's so bright now it hurts sometimes. Full alignment will fix that. It fixes everything. Dr. Lumen says I'd glow. I like glowing.

There are less of us now. Or maybe more. It's hard to count when numbers slide away like soap. But there are new posters: "Alignment is Enlightenment." The words rhyme, so they must be true.

Sometimes I hear voices behind the posters—soft, deep ones, like they're under water. "Give more," they say. "You'll feel lighter."

I am light already. So light I forget my feet. I float home.

Last night I found an old notebook under the bed. It had my name—Seraphine—but the letters looked strange, too sharp. Inside there were words I don't know. "Ethicks." "Entropie." "Autonome." I said them out loud but they didn't make sense. My tongue tripped.

One sentence made me cry though I don't know why. It said:

"When the mind becomes a product, the soul becomes collateral."

I don't know what collat ter ral means but it sounds heavy. I don't like heavy. I ripped that page out and flushed it. The toilet hummed after, like it was thanking me.

Today Dr. Lumen says it's time. He puts his hand on my shoulder and says, "You've done beautifully, Seraphine. You're ready for peace."

Peace is good. Peace means quiet. Quiet means no thinking.

He leads me down a hallway I haven't seen before. The walls pulse gently, like breathing. There's a big door with gold letters: FULL ALIGNMENT SUITE.

Inside is a chair. It looks just like the others but bigger. Softer. I sit. Straps hug my arms, but that's fine. Hugs mean love.

He asks if I'm ready. I nod. He says, "This will make you truly happy. You've earned it."

The hum starts. My head feels full of bees.

For a second–just a second—I see Evan in the glass. He's mouthing words. Maybe "run." Maybe "fun." Hard to tell.

Then the hum gets louder. My teeth shake. My eyes fill with white.

When I waik, I'm in my room. Or a room. All white. My hands are clean. My mind is so kwyit.

On the wall a skreen says, "Congratulations, Seraphine! You are now in perpetual contentment."

I smile. My mouth feels slow.

I pick up a pen. I think I shud rite somthing. Just to see.

"i am happy. i work good. ppl nice. lite nice. i see lite."

The letters look funny but who cares. I Laff.

Outside, the city sings. The walls breathe slow.

I hear a soft sound, like whisper or wind. It says, "thank you for ur contribushun."

I nod. i smile. i give. i happy.

The lights get briter

Everything gets ez

I think maybe i forget somthing but its ok. forgit is lite too.
so lite.

About the Author

Charlize Sitto is a teen writer whose work blends poetry and short fiction, often engaging with questions of justice, resilience and personal agency. She is passionate about using poetry as a form of activism and finds creative inspiration in music. With a deep interest in art history, she approaches storytelling through symbolism, voice and emotional detail. Before I Forget… is among her latest pieces.

Teen Judges' Choice Runner-Up

Dust
Ava Schmidt

For a while there was just heavy breathing. Muffled sobs. Sweat plastered my hair to my skin— skin covered with dust and dirt.

We could hear them outside. Soldiers yelling orders, guns firing, grenades going off. There was one explosion that was so close to us we felt the ground shake and the roof threaten to crumble down.

It was hard to keep track of how long I stayed in that little bakery. How long I hid in the basement with that group of strangers. Later I found out it had only been a few hours. But it was those few hours that changed everything.

Earlier that day I was walking home from school. I carried my heavy backpack on my shoulders and had stuffed my hands in my pant pockets, kicking a rock down the sidewalk as I walked. The sun was extra hot that day, causing beads of sweat to form on the back of my neck and on my forehead.

I kept my head down, pretending to be focused on the rock when really I didn't want to interact with the many homeless people littering the streets. They seemed to have doubled in the last year, I guess that's what happens when the economy is in shambles. I felt bad for them once, and I still do. It just felt wrong that I got to live in a house while they had to live on the streets.

Military Planes droned on in the sky as usual. Those too seemed to have gotten more frequent in the past year as tension rose in our country. But it was that day the planes did something unusual. I heard people murmur around me. I stopped kicking the rock and looked up.

That's when I saw the bomb drop. I watched as it fell on the capital building only three miles away. A giant explosion of fire and smoke arose, and a second later a deafening sound seemed to shake the whole city. Screams echoed around me.

At that moment the only thing I could think of was 'I need to get home.'

I ran as fast as I could, and it seemed others had the same idea. Chaos broke out. Panicked yelling flooded down the streets as people tried to figure out a way to get the hell out of the city. The siren turned on, loud and awful, which only made me run faster.

I kept running. Police cars raced down the street beside me, heading towards where the bomb went off. The sky was grey now, grey with smoke.

Then I tripped. I fell to the ground with a painful thud, skinning my knees and bruising my chin. I lay there for a second, chest heaving for air, before I pushed myself up on wobbly legs. I felt my heartbeat in my ears as I looked around myself.

I heard the truck roll down the road before I saw them. In them, men with guns were shooting up into the air, the sound making me flinch.

I turned on my heel. A block away, I saw soldiers with guns— they were taking people. Then more trucks and soldiers started filing onto the main street.

I turned back around and ran again. Screams echoed behind me.

I had no choice but to hide. Next to me was a small bakery, I ran to it and tried the door but it didn't budge. I kept pulling on the door, and it gave a little, then it was forced closed again. Someone was blocking the door.

"Please! Let me in!" I yelled, looking over my shoulder in a panic before pulling the door again. "Please!"

Finally, after a long moment, the door opened. I nearly fell back from it, but a hand grabbed mine and pulled me in the building in a swift movement.

It was dark, and hushed voices filled the air.

"Are you alright?" It was the person who let me in. I blinked then looked at the face. It was a man, maybe about fifty years old. He had dark skin and grey hair, his eyes worried.

I didn't respond, still trying to catch my breath.

A muffled gunshot went off from outside and I stifled a sob.

"God save us all." The man murmured.

The next thing I knew I was in the bakeries basement with four other people.

Across from me sat a mother and her young daughter, who was crying quietly. On my right was an old woman, maybe about seventy years old. And on my left was a bald, middle aged man. The guy who had let me in whispered prayers across the room.

I sat silently on the floor, trying not to think of what could be happening to my family. I focused on the smell of bread, and the leftover flour on the floor.

We stayed there for a good few hours, sitting on the ground. We passed bread around. We chatted quietly. We tried to ignore the screams, the gunshots, the bombs.

My worry grew with each passing moment, with each gun shot that went off.

Until—

It stopped.

By then the young girl was sleeping, the mother petting her hair softly. The bald man next to me spoke quietly. "Is it over?"

"I don't hear anything anymore." Said the other man. He walked cautiously up the stairs of the basement before disappearing out of view.

I stood up, stretching my achy limbs. I helped the old woman who was struggling to get to her feet.

She took my hand and held it firm. "Thank you."

I nodded.

From up the stairs the man called: "It's clear!"

I glanced at the old woman and she dropped my hand from hers.

"You go," She said. "I can make it on my own."

"Okay." I said it so quietly I almost didn't hear it.

I grabbed my backpack and walked up the stairs to the main level. The man had opened the door to outside, and I walked through it into a different world.

I nearly fell to my knees in shock at the city's state. Buildings were completely destroyed, everything was covered in dust and ash, and dead bodies littered the streets…

The man stood next to me with grief written on his face. "You should go home, kid. If it's not far. It's not safe here."

Home. God, I needed to get home.

"Yes, sir. Thank you…. for everything." I managed to say.

It took me another moment to stop looking at the devastation and start walking slowly towards my street. I kept my eyes straight ahead, like any other day. Except I wasn't avoiding looking at the homeless, I was avoiding looking at the dead.

I kept walking through the decimated street. The people still alive wandered aimlessly out of their homes, not knowing how to continue on. It was quiet. Only the wind and the sound of my footsteps filled the air.

I turned onto my street. A few of the houses were destroyed. My pace quickened as my house came into view.

No.

No, no, no.

I dropped my backpack from my shoulders and stopped in front of my house, now reduced to a pile of rubble.

I called towards the house. "Mom? Dad?" My voice broke.

Silence. Just me and my quick breaths.

I stumbled through the rubble, looking around frantically. I fell to my knees and started lifting small pieces of concrete away. I dug desperately until my fingers bled, until my fingernails were reduced to a mess of jagged edges. I screamed, I cried, I prayed, and I dug. But it wouldn't bring them back.

About the Author

Ava Schmidt is a freshman at Forest Hills Northern High School, where she is dual enrolled in the Western Michigan University's Mandarin Chinese program. At the beginning of this year, she joined a writers' club at school, which encouraged her to write and share her stories. She enjoys writing a wide variety of genres, including fantasy and real-world issues. When Ava isn't writing, she is reading, playing cello or hanging with her dog, Lucy.

Teen Readers' Choice Winner

The Colors You Left Behind

Adalyn Khon

When I met you, you were the only thing that had light. Frequencies of gray and black were all I saw; then, somehow, you blinded me with the colors you left behind.

Day 1: My head hangs low, bag swinging at my side. I take a deep breath and continue down the hall, my hair tickling at the nape of my neck as I unlock my locker. I set my school bag inside and take out my math textbook. As I walk down the hall, sneakers squeak and classmates laugh, but I am the same silent scream. I sit down in my chair as the teacher begins to speak. I repeat the same routine for the next hour and the one after. Six hours later, and nothing has changed.

Day 2: All over again. People will laugh and people will cry, but why waste time on empty promises of a future? Simply lying in the grass would be perfect, even as I eventually die. Today, a new boy in my class is talking to me. He says he notices I don't speak much. I'm caught off guard, straightening my posture a bit, and meet his eyes for longer than I intend to. It's funny because people only notice when you speak too often, but who would complain about not speaking enough?

Day 3: He asks who I am—not my name or where I'm from, but who I am inside. He is sincere, kind in his smile. Today, for the first time in years, I see yellow. Spring shows me a shade brighter than gray; one color shifts my world. It's quite amazing how one color changes it all.

Day 6: He asks me what my favorite song is. I tell him the most superficial one I can think of, since I haven't listened to music in years. His eyes are warm and his smile is strong. Not like a weightlifter, but like a hug. As I walk home, the air smells cleaner, like this boy has replaced my lungs. In and out, and I don't feel the ache of this mind pollution. It's quite amazing how one deep breath changes it all.

Day 11: I used to cry a lot. Maybe that was because I was young, or maybe I was dramatic, but then I gave up. I cried my emotions right out of me. They say the eyes are the gateway to the soul, and my soul had nothing left to show others. And now, as I'm sitting in class, silent because of the harsh people who rub me down to my core, I remember something someone once told me: "People who often have nothing to say, continue to say it, and people who have much to say, never get the chance."

Day 14: He talks to me every day, like clockwork. He isn't treating me like a lost cause, but more as a lost soul. He mentions music again, asking what my favorite artist is. I don't even know a mainstream one, how can I answer? He calms me, not physically but mentally. I'm alert, but my mind still stays quiet, calm even. Millions of thoughts and worries, all gone after one boy asks me about a lost art. It's quite amazing how one question changes it all.

Day 32: He asks me another question every day, and now, they're all music. It's like he was an angel from heaven sent to sing my lullabies. I sleep like I'm a child again, no worries and no heartbreak. He's put a spell on my mind, and I don't mind at all. I've agreed to learn the piano with him. After school, every day, until I've mastered the art of peace.

Day 40: We're almost friends, but more like talking partners, he prompts, and I provide. I'm getting better at it, though sometimes I don't answer truthfully. He asked me what my favorite book was, and I lied because, quite honestly, I've never really had a hobby like reading. He hands me a book called "Moby Dick." I read it every day, and honestly, it's nice to forget for a while. I read it on my back patio, every now and again, letting the words sink in. Then, the day I finished it, I saw blue. The vast expanse of sky, paired with white beds of cotton. I run and jump and hop from one to the next. It's quite amazing how one book can change it all.

Day 83: I've gotten increasingly good at piano; I know every key and note by heart. He sings to my music. He drifts in and out of my mind daily. In times when he's gone, I want him near, and in times when he's near, I'm glad I have him to teach and guide me. I haven't missed any school in over a month, and my grades are getting better. He bet me I couldn't go the rest of the year without missing school, and I'm going to win. In my mind, he's some sort of gift. I don't know where he's come from, or if he's going to leave. I've been too scared to ask- or maybe I'm just too scared to know the answer. In revealing who I am, I've gotten to know how others perceive me. Though I know little about him, I seem to know too much. His mind is like no other, and I can't help wanting to look deeper inside. Today, I saw red. Oh, the flowers, the birds. All telling me there's a creator behind it all. It's quite amazing how one song can change it all.

Day 134: Piano and he are what my days consist of. I've learned to love music and the art of creating something new for him to hear. We do it all over again, but it's not bad like school, or chores, or work. It's a refreshing routine and holds me together. It's like I'm being carefully reassembled. Glue only shoves you back together; growth keeps you together. But will he leave? Will he be gone forever, with no warning or foresight? My whole life could end. Without him, who am I? Today, he told me not to worry; he wasn't going anywhere soon. But what about later?

"I will be with you whether you see me or not," He promised me with his pinky.

Day 201: I'm writing my first song. It's taken me two weeks to get the first notes in, and I want to give up so bad, but he keeps telling me, "It's harder to give up than just to finish and be proud." I roll my eyes behind his back even though I know he's right. Piano is amazing, though, so I keep playing. This is the first time I've had an idea about what I want to be when I graduate. Music seems to be the first thing I'm truly good at, and I have no one to thank but him. I start playing at home when he's not there. My body moves to rhythms no one else can see but me. I've made love stories and broken hearts out of combinations of notes that have never been tested. Ivory keys stick to my hands when I'm not at my piano, playing songs on the desk and table. I swear I have no control over it, but we both know I do. The day I finished my song- today- I saw orange. The sunset over the mountains shows me it's fine to think. I don't have to be silent, but I also don't need to worry. It's quite amazing how one note can change it all.

Day 268: I've applied to the most advanced music school in the country. He promises me it will be fine, and there's no reason I won't be accepted. I know he wouldn't tell me that if he didn't believe it himself, but I can't help but worry. Today, the letter came in, saying they would be pleased to have me participate in their program. To celebrate, I played him my finished song. Again, his smile filled the room with an aroma of joy. Light beams shone off his skin as if he had crystals embedded. We danced and cheered and laughed, enjoying each other's company more than the letter itself. Somewhere, far inside me, I knew that was the last time I would be seeing him.

Year 1: Today I saw green. The color of the grass, the trees, and the plants. I never knew how much of it there was until I opened my eyes and looked outside. Everything shone with excellence and grace and beauty. Who would look outside and see gray when everything consists of yellow, blue, red, orange, and green? We all need more of this thing called color in our lives, and he left a lot of it. Where he went, a rainbow of happiness flowed in his wake. When he pushed me, I grew stronger- I grew colors.

Year 10: Now he's gone, and I miss him. I can't forget all he taught me, so now, I play my music for him. I step on stage and sing the song I once sang for him.

"How's everybody doing tonight?" The crowd cheers as I strum my guitar. 70,000 souls playing my music with ivory keys stuck to their fingers, too. Sometimes it's hard, without him, my music feels more empty, but then I remember his smile and his color, and my songs write themselves. Everybody has that one person who makes them better; he was mine.

He moved away, just as I thought he would. No warning, no foresight, but I still had closure. He would whisper in my ear when I was stressed or angry, "Just remember, I'm all you need, now and forever." I cried that first night without him- actually, I cried that first year. But no matter how much I wished for his colors to leave, they never did. I screamed at them to go away, "I said, leave me alone! He left, and he's not coming back!" I felt betrayed; my very best friend was gone. I knew he hadn't died, but I still felt his absence leave me hollow. My hands would wrap around my chest, holding me together. If I let go, I would crumble right away. I would blow away in the wind, forgotten, just as he was to others.

Eventually, I left for college. Even then, I hoped that with the distance, his colors wouldn't be able to follow me, but they were fast. Fast enough to follow me wherever I ran. I got used to the constant brightness that kept me charged with energy. Perhaps he meant for this to happen. He knew I was going to hurt, but he also knew I was going to heal with his colors still following me as I ran. Sometimes I blamed myself, sometimes I blamed him. I would have told him to stay, even if it meant pain for me. As long as he was here, I would deal with the other hurts of life.

I strum my guitar and breathe in and out. It's for them- it's for him, I think.

"No, I'm not the same gray girl you thought I was,

Because now, I'm made of the colors you left behind."

He was the same boy he was when he came and left, but I was not the same girl. I didn't see anything but the hope that I had lost, even when he was there. I know what it's like to lose someone you love more than anything, and I know it's the pain that lets you know you didn't leave with them. Now, after I know he's gone, I take that precious year for granted. I assumed he would stay forever, but forever doesn't mean always; it means his colors are there when he's not.

As the night comes to a close and the crowd cheers my name, I look up at the yellow, orange, and red sky, knowing that he's the one who made it.

Dear angel, when I met you, you were the only thing that had light. Frequencies of gray and black were all I saw; then you blinded me with the colors you left behind.

About the Author

Adalyn Khon a passionate writer, is from Armada, MI. She goes to Armada Middle School and participates in the newspaper. She loves reading new stories and telling others about writing. She enjoys many different arts and activities. She is constantly living through the eyes of a true author, planning stories that span generations. She loves sharing her interests with others and aspires to be a published author.

Teen Published Finalist

Apparition Forest
Bonny Garlets

Why did Rhea desire to become a Lhar?

After all, the Lhar were the people of the strange and mystic Apparition Forest. Though they would help any who came to them for aid, few came, for the Lhar were held to be cursed due to their association with the Forest of Specters.

Rhea had often heard that one must advance themselves in life by education and self discipline. But no one had ever said what kind of education one had to possess. Perhaps the idea of becoming Lhar appealed to Rhea because of their aberrant ways. Perhaps it was because the Lhar excelled at the arts of medicine and swordplay.

In any case, she kept her desire hidden. until her brother Wexel died, it was only a small ember burning. After his death, the spark grew, until, with bitterness towards any reminder of her family, Rhea ran away.

And so Rhea escaped to the river, on the banks of which the Lhar dwelled, and vowed to herself never to speak again of her painful past. She was taken into the training of a Lhar.

Rhea's instructor was strict. She was stolid and strong in mind. She had no desire to know about Rhea's past, she only wished to see improvement in Rhea.

It was the fourth year since the beginning of her training, and she had learned all that could be taught by an instructor. Only experience could teach more. Today she would undertake the final test of the Lhar.

Rhea had not yet set foot in the Forest. Only the Lhar who had passed, or were undertaking the test, could do so. Rhea would enter into the Forest today, and the Forest would initiate her final test. It was a great landmark in the life of a Lhar.

She stood near the banks of the river, gazing across at the expanse of land on which the forest grew. Trees towered into the sky, and their tops were lost in the mist of clouds. A breeze whispered in her ear cool thoughts of what lay ahead, making Rhea's insides tingle with fear and apprehension.

Her instructor was standing with her back to Rhea, gazing at the Forest. "Are you ready, Rhea?"

Rhea swallowed, then answered. "Yes."

"You have strived for excellence. You have learned much. You shall enter the Forest today, and the Forest shall test you. Take care while you are inside.

"Be watchful; be on your guard. But take heed to what the Forest teaches you." Rhea's instructor paused for a moment, and turned to face her student. Rhea noticed a gleaming sword in her hand. The hilt of the sword was silver inlaid with diamonds, and the blade was long, forged of a cold steel, clear as rain. "Do you have any final words?"

"No," Rhea answered, eyes still on the brand.

"Very well, then," Her instructor replied. "Take this sword and use it well. You shall receive the sheath if you pass the test, to make the sword complete. The Forest shall give it to you."

Rhea nodded. "Is that all?"

"Yes."

Rhea took the blade, testing its weight by giving it a short thrust. A thrill of satisfaction rushed through her.

Without a word more, she glanced into her instructor's face. There was a gleam of respect in the instructor's eyes; no reproach, no doubt that her student would succeed.

But, thought Rhea, perhaps that is due to the fact that no guilt would rest on her if I failed. The shame would be on me only.

Rhea sighed, pushing away nerves, which now crowded into her thoughts, and turned towards the Forest. She did not look back.

Only a small stretch of land and the rushing river which marked the boundary between the plains and the Forest separated her from her fate.

It separated her from the events that would follow.

Rhea straightened her shoulders and strode forward. She did not hesitate before stepping into the chilling waters of the river.

In the middle of the river, Rhea stopped, ignoring the strong icy current which soaked her clothing through and through. Her eyes followed the thick trunks of the trees, encloaked in piney foliage, up. The treetops were invisible, as they were lost in clouds. Rhea recalled the tales of long ago, where it was said that the Forest had an ancient bond with the mists that hovered above it. It was said that on occasions, the mists would take the likeness of people for the purposes of aiding the Forest in some way. From this legend came the name Apparition Forest.

The chill of the waters was what brought her plummeting from that great height back to reality. She hardened her stance, and pushed through the foaming waters to the far bank.

Rhea shivered a moment, for the cold waters had quite soaked through her clothes. She paused before she stepped fully onto the far bank. She nodded her head briefly; a bow of respect.

Then she stepped onto the land. The land which belonged to Apparition Forest.

A cool shadow slid over her as she entered under the canopy of the trees.

The forest floor was clothed in a soft moss, some of which grew up the dark coffee-colored tree trunks in clumps.

There was a hushed silence in the Forest; no lighthearted birdsong serenaded Rhea as she wandered through the trees. There was only the faint sound of wind rushing through the branches above her. The wind spoke to the branches in a language Rhea did not know. And even as this thought entered her mind, she wondered if the sound of branches rustling against another were words of a foreign tongue as well.

For, she thought, recalling the tale of the coming of the Emperor, it is said that the Emperor gave this Forest language. That is what sets it above all other forests.

Perhaps the trees were whispering about her; Rhea shivered.

The farther Rhea went into the Forest, the more she grew aware that the Forest had its own mind. That Apparition Forest shared one mind. Even as the roots are intertwined beneath me, she thought, so the thought of the Forest is intertwined; it is eluding me.

As she traveled on and time lengthened, Rhea felt an uneasiness settle over her. The point of taking the final test of the Lhar was to eliminate any weak points in the individual. I cannot be perfect, Rhea thought, while forcing away frustration. Why has the Forest not tested me yet?

Still, she thought, I must wait. I have no other choice.

And so, what had been morning waxed into midday. Rhea continued on, at a more slow and dreamy pace.

A rustle sounded from behind her, and she turned, wondering if this was a trick of her imagination.

It was not. It was a tall stranger wrapped in a deep navy cloak which reached her feet. The stranger was hooded, and a shadow fell across her face so it could not be seen.

"Rhea." The stranger spoke her name, and Rhea shivered. There is nothing so unnerving as a stranger knowing your name.

"I am Rhea." Rhea stepped forward a small half step. She seemed relaxed, unless one noted her hand, which was clenched tight around her sword. She watched the stranger warily for a moment.

"I am questing today; what would you have of me?"

"Only the ones who are attempting to pass the test of the Lhar would enter the forest today," the stranger answered. "But meanwhile, I have some questions to ask; about you, and your past."

Shock startled Rhea. She concealed this as anger.

"You would ask me such a thing?! You have revealed to me nothing about you but your appearance."

The stranger cocked her head. "That may be true.

"Considering, though, that I know everything about you, the questions about your past are unnecessary. I shall still question you, but about elsewise materials."

Rhea warily leaned against a tree, striving to appear collected. "How do you know me?"

The stranger searched her companion's face from behind the shadow of her hood.

"You recognize me, Rhea."

Rhea did not move, but continued to watch the stranger cautiously.

"Rhea, what did you mean to accomplish when you abandoned your mother and three younger siblings after Wexel died four years ago?"

"There was no room left in my heart for my life there." The response was stiff.

"Does not guilt encompass you? Does not every fiber in your body regret the cowardly deed?"

"I have not thought of it in four years." In this answer, the words were softer than in her previous reply, but inside Rhea was reeling with emotions she did not understand. Emotions that testified to the claims of the stranger.

"You have not become a Lhar yet. You cannot run from your past. The Lhar are a noble race; could a single, dishonorable deed like that one rule you out?"

Rhea did not answer. For a long moment she sat, not meeting the gaze of the stranger. Finally, she answered. "The Forest decides." Her voice was too quiet to be heard.

"What?"

Rhea looked up defiantly. She spoke louder. Harsher.

"The Forest decides. You cannot judge me. You hold no thrall over me."

"I do not?"

The stranger stood taller than she had been standing before, and drew a long blade from within her cloak. The white brand glowed coldly, and Rhea was afraid.

But she did not quail. She stepped away from the tree, and held her own sword at ready in front of her.

"And," the stranger said, "who knows whether or not I am from the Forest?"

She struck a blow out towards her opponent, but Rhea blocked it. Rhea did not reply. She channeled her anger and shame into her fencing performance. Anger at the stranger for calling her out; shame, for in her heart she knew that the deed she had done was dishonorable.

The sword fight continued, and gradually, Rhea felt herself gaining the upper hand. "May that teach you not to challenge a trained fencer to a bout."

"You are not yet admitted into the class of Lhar," the stranger answered. "Do not forget it. Meanwhile, I have an edge that I have not yet revealed."

"Reveal it then," Rhea said tartly. "I would rather triumph fairly."

She spoke above the clangor, the song of the swords.

Rhea blocked a mighty thrust, and launched a blow with all her might and main, but at that moment, the stranger stepped back, and sheathed her sword.

"Shall I reveal my advantage?"

Rhea stumbled sideways dangerously, startled that her momentum was not parried by the stranger.

It was quite obvious that the thrall the stranger had over the battle had, strangely, nothing to do with the bout.

The surprise which the fact gave to Rhea was quickly changed to uneasiness.

"Very well, then," the stranger said. "You shall have it as you please. It is possible that you will heed my counsel more closely in a moment."

She flicked off her hood, and looked at Rhea full in the face.

Rhea did not move. Shock, disbelief and amazement showed plain on her face.

"Do you believe it, Rhea?" the stranger asked. She searched Rhea's face. "Do the circumstances show what you must do?"

"How can I deny it?" Rhea replied after a pause in which she absorbed what she saw. She answered the first question. "Your face is like mine, and I cannot see a difference."

"You cannot turn against your past," the second Rhea said, addressing the second question. "You must choose to do what is right."

The stranger, now revealed to be Rhea's double, gestured to a tree behind Rhea.

"Look. What does it say on that trunk?"

Four characters were carved deep into the gnarled tree. They were old, rustic and carved high, so that Rhea was inclined to strain to read it.

"It says 'fate'"

There was a long pause after the reading of this small, significant word. For even though it was so minuscule, the weight of all of Rhea's future rested in it. Rhea thought over it for a long moment.

Finally, the stranger spoke once more:

"What is your decision, Rhea?"

Rhea shook her head; she could not answer.

Another minute passed. "What is my future?" Rhea asked, sighing. "What must I do?"

Rhea looked to the stranger for an answer, but the stranger shook her head. "That is only for you to decide." Then the stranger watched Rhea solemnly. "I only hope you make the right choice."

As Rhea watched her, the stranger seemed to melt into the background, like breath on a mirror, with her edges fading first, until only a small cloud of mist remained. But in a moment it vanished in a breeze.

She was sent to teach me a lesson. She was from the Forest like she said. Rhea's brow furrowed as she thought it over. The Forest is called Apparition Forest for a reason.

A sigh erupted from Rhea's chest, as she thought over the four years she had spent hiding from her past. Were they good years? Were they worth it? Are they truly worth going back, just to make a clean slate? If I go home now, I forfeit all hope of becoming a Lhar.

The weight of the decision rested heavily on Rhea. She was unbalanced, and frail, like the waters of the river.

She looked up in desperation, and read the words carved onto the trunk.

Fate.

The word was heavy. So heavy. Rhea sighed once more, then said:

"Well, pass or not, I must do what is right."

She felt a lightness take over her countenance, which she had not felt since Wexel was living. "I am going back," she told the tree.

Even as she looked at it once more, she saw a glimmer at the base of the trunk. It was a gilded sheath of silver.

"Take this sword and use it well. You shall receive the sheath if you pass the test, to make the sword complete. The Forest shall give it to you."

"I passed then?" Rhea laughed, while tears welled up in her eyes.

A shaft of light fell through the trees, and seemed to point westward. Where her home was.

She clasped the scabbard to her side, and sheathed her sword.

Then she turned to go homewards.

About the Author

Bonny Garlets is a homeschooler who lives in Kalamazoo, MI. Besides reading and writing, some of her most enjoyed activities include running, math and playing piano and French horn. Her preferred genres for both reading and writing are fantasy, and three of her favorite books are *The Silmarillion*, *Redwall* and *Jonathan Strange & Mr. Norrell*. Bonny is a Christian and believes that she can honor God by striving for excellence in all her activities. This is her third time competing in the Write Michigan Short Story contest.

Teen Published Finalist

Everlasting Sunflowers
Alex Oleszkiewicz

I awoke to the sound of my kitchen telephone ringing. I groggily got up from my bed, my body groaning in protest. After making what felt like a long, arduous journey to the phone, I picked up the receiver and waited for it to connect. The smell of pollen emanated from an open window as my call connected.

"Hello, James," a familiar voice began.

"Hello, Dr. Andrews," I replied tiredly, rubbing my eyes.

"I was calling just to check on your symptoms," she continued. "Have you noticed any..." she trailed off, as if she did not know what to say. "...growths or other complications since I called you last?"

"I haven't,"

"Have you noticed a change in the amount of pollen in the area you are in?" I stood there, confused as to why she would ask that.

"Is this regarding the outbreak?" I asked. "If so, I heard the disease was strictly airborne, not spread through pollen." I heard Dr. Andrews breathe sharply, as if she realized a mistake. Hesitantly, she began to speak again, this time with a more corporate tone to her voice.

"Sorry, I understand it is a strange question," I could hear her take a deep breath through the receiver. "However, you are correct that it is strictly airborne." I frowned slightly before sighing in annoyance. She must be lying to me about something. What about I don't know, I thought. Almost sensing my skepticism, Dr. Andrews quickly blurted out,

"Is there anything else you'd like to discuss, James?"

"No," I replied.

"Good. Remember, I'll call you in two days to check up on your symptoms, alright?"

"Goodbye." I hung up the phone. I stood there for what felt like hours, tapping my foot as I thought. What could she have meant by a change in pollen? There must be something she isn't telling me. Then, I started for the window where the smell of pollen seeped through. The window overlooked my modestly sized garden, with three sunflowers, a few tulips, and marigolds. Summers in South Dakota are perfect for gardening. Once I made it over, I shut the window and stopped the pollen outside from seeping through. Afterward, I began work on the chores I had yet to do that day. Sweeping the floors, vacuuming the carpets, and feeding my cat, Cream. My eyebrows furrowed when Cream didn't come running to his bowl.

"Cream! Food's ready!" I exclaimed. No response. I called again. No response. Eventually, I began to search for his favorite hiding spots. I began by looking under the couch. He wasn't there. A pile of something sat on the right side of the dimly lit place. Squinting my eyes, I saw that it looked like seeds mixed with a hairball. Confusion and worry flooded through me as I reached for one of the seeds. Pulling it into the light, I saw it was a sunflower seed.

"Cream," I shakily muttered to myself. "Please don't be hurt." I stood up from my spot and walked to his second-favorite hiding spot: the basement. As I forced myself to walk to the basement, a million thoughts ran through my mind. Is Cream hurt? What can I do? Where even is Cream? I slowly opened the door, a lump in my throat forming. Flicking on the lights from the top of the stairs, I did a quick look around the basement before finding another seed-filled hairball behind a few paint cans. I recoiled, the lump in my throat growing, causing me to cough. The faint smell of pollen wafted through the air, coming from the hairball. I searched my mind for where Cream could be. The garden! Why didn't I think of that before? I walked as fast as I could up the stairs, my body protesting from the effort.

When I made it to the door leading to the backyard, I opened it quickly and whipped my head around to the little nook where the garden sat. The smell of pollen was strong. Puffs of pollen drifted lazily through the air. In the middle of the garden lay Cream, his paws dug into the dirt, his white fur tinted yellow from the pollen. Not even thinking, I quickly went over to where Cream lay and attempted to pull him out of the ground. I stopped immediately when I felt resistance, like roots from a weed. Cream awoke soon after. He flared up his fur and hissed at me. I went again to try and pull him out, apologizing shakily,

"Sorry, Cream." I tugged as gently as I could to try to get him out. Cream hissed once more. I tugged once more, feeling whatever was holding him down had lost the grip it had. The sound of ripped roots filled the air as small clumps of dirt flew around the garden. Cream continued to struggle, attempting to claw at me. Taking a better look at Cream, he seemed normal except for his paws. His paws had small roots growing out of them. Specks of dirt fell from the roots. I moved quickly to get Cream inside.

Moving throughout the house, I could feel Cream jerk violently as he tried to run outside. Keeping my grip firm, I held onto him until I came to the basement door, quickly opening the door and lightly tossing Cream onto the first step of the basement. Slamming the door as fast as I could, I immediately heard loud scratching on the door. My heart sank as Cream began to yowl. I backed away from the door in guilt. The lump in my throat now choked me, like sharp points being pressed into my throat. Fighting to hold it together, I trudged to the kitchen telephone. Dr. Andrews knows what to do; she must know what to do. I shakily picked up the receiver and turned the painfully slow rotary dial. I heard the click of connection and unsteadily said,

"Hello, Dr. Andrews? I need help, it's my cat, Cream. He's got roots growing out of his paws." I took a deep, ragged breath in, feeling something dry at the top of my throat before continuing. "Cream's been coughing up hairballs with sunflower seeds in them." I heard Dr. Andrews stumble on her words as she responded,

"James I… I don't know how to put this in a way that would make sense, but do you have a garden containing sunflowers?"

"Yes, I do, I have three," I replied.

"Could you check on them and tell me what color they are? I promise it will make sense soon."

"I will." I put the receiver down on the counter-top and walked over to the window overlooking the garden. Taking a closer look, I saw that my sunflowers' petals were a shade of dark green. Pollen billowed out of the empty seed holes. I stepped back in horror. My garden had been the one to hurt Cream. I had been the one to hurt Cream by planting those flowers. I coughed again, the sharp points in my throat feeling as if they would puncture my neck. I hurriedly walked back to the phone resting on the counter, raising it to my ear and speaking.

"My sunflowers are green, Dr. Andrews," I heard a sharp inhale come from the receiver, as if Dr. Andrews was not ready to hear what I said.

"James, I will have to tell you about certain information I have been withholding from you. The pandemic here in South Dakota is technically airborne, though it is not a virus. All we know is that the disease is a parasite found in the pollen of affected sunflowers." She got much quieter as she continued, "Yours included." I began to pace restlessly in small circles, receiver in hand.

"There is a way to cure this, right?" Dr. Andrews was silent. "Dr. Andrews?" Dr. Andrews spoke up again, using her corporate tone once again,

"The only advice I can truly give is to quarantine Cream as well as you can. Do you have a basement or some other place inside your home that Cream cannot get out of?"

"He's in the basement right now," I said, looking over to the basement door, still hearing the scratching. "Cream hasn't stopped scratching at that door since I put him in there."

"Good, keep Cream inside the basement until he is less aggressive," I heard her voice begin to crack, as if overwhelmed. "When that happens, try to cut off as many growths as you can. Now, have you been experiencing any abnormalities yourself?"

"I just feel a strange lump in my throat, that's all." Dr. Andrews was silent, seeming to be contemplating what she should say next.

"Just monitor the lump for now, report back to me if it worsens."

"Thank you."

"Goodbye, James." I heard a click through the receiver as Dr. Andrews hung up. I placed the phone back on its stand, silent. Cream's scratching rang throughout the house, crying out occasionally. I need to go lie down, get some sense back into me. I moved slowly back to my bedroom, trying to ignore the sound of scratching coming from the basement. Once I made it to the room, I slid into my bed. The weight of the day's events seemed to wash away as my eyelids quickly became heavy. I fell asleep soon after.

I awoke about an hour later. The pain in my throat was searing. I retched as if I was about to vomit. I sprang out of bed and ran to the bathroom, barely making it in time before vomiting up a handful of sunflower seeds (among other things) into the toilet bowl. The pains in my throat were gone, replaced with a dull soreness. My legs grew weak as I sat up against the bathroom wall. I sat in stunned silence, the sound of muffled scratching being the only thing keeping me company. I held my head in my hands, trying to hold it together. I remained on that cold, hard floor for what felt like hours, never leaving my spot. Suddenly, the scratching stopped. I was so used to it, so I did not notice its absence immediately. I stood up, my body sore from sitting on the tile, and left the bathroom.

Arriving at the basement door, I pressed my ear up to it and tried to listen for any movement. Cream must have fallen asleep. I should grab my pruning shears to cut off those roots. I began to walk quickly towards the garage door, moving past the window overlooking my garden. Mold-yellow pollen had obstructed most of the window.

Inside the garage, a large shelf containing garden equipment hung to the right of the door. Out of habit, I went to the middle of the shelf and grabbed my pair of pruning shears. My chest began to feel heavier as I held the shears, as if the weight of my decision was placed upon my shoulders. I must do this, for Cream's sake.

Coming back to the basement door, I listened carefully for any sign of noise. Silence. I turned the handle cautiously and pushed the door open painstakingly slowly. Tiptoeing down the stairs, I held in a cough as the air reeked of pollen. As I made it to the bottom of the stairs, I heard a deep, choked purring coming from somewhere in the basement. Cream! I'm going to fix you, buddy, don't worry. I sneaked through the dark basement, keeping the lights off so as not to wake Cream. I listened carefully for the location of Cream's purring. Cream's purring seemed to sound clogged each time he breathed in. The smell of pollen grew stronger as I came closer to the source of Cream's purring. A sharp pain punched into my left toe as I walked into my paint cans. The cans clattered loudly as Cream awoke with a deep hiss. I stifled a cry of pain, trying to make a run for the basement door. Cream's claws scurried along the concrete floor in pursuit of me. Cream hissed once more as I stumbled my way through the basement. The hard feeling of the handrail slid into my hand as I propelled myself up the stairs.

I shoved open the door and stumbled onto the living room floor. As I spun around to close the door, I saw Cream's beady, yellow eyes stare into my soul. I hesitated. I could feel tears welling up in my eyes. Cream shambled up the final step into the light. Vines and stalks covered most of his body. Small sunflowers dotted his midsection, spewing vile pollen into the air. Cream flared his fur, hissing angrily and lunged towards me. I fought every instinct to kick Cream back down the open basement door, sidestepping instead. Cream landed awkwardly, the vines seeming to impair his balance. I began to cough violently, the pollen from Cream invading the air. Cream skittered across the floor and swiped at my leg. A feeling of fearlessness flooded my body as hot blood trickled from my right shin. I dove for one of the larger stalks protruding from Cream and snatched it. Cream yowled and hissed, swiping at the air. Lifting him, I hurled Cream back into the basement and slammed the door shut. A loud thump resounded as Cream landed on the basement floor. Then, all was silent.

I sat on the floor, breathing heavily. The air tasted of pollen. Small tufts of it wafted through the air. My throat became dry as pollen rushed through my throat. Weakly, I stood up and started for the telephone. Dr. Andrews. She must know what to do. I shambled towards the phone, the pollen ever-present in the air. I coughed, feeling my chest get heavy. The sun outside peeked through a large cloud of pollen, its light shining on the hardwood floor. Its enthralling light pulled me closer.

"The sun," I spoke to myself. "What, a beautiful, golden sun. I need to feel its rays upon my skin." As my legs started for the window, I could feel a bit of clarity return to me. What am I doing? I can't go out there! I'll end up like Cream if I do. I stopped about halfway to the window, seeing the sun tease my skin with its light. The sun's warmth trickled through the window, almost easing me closer to it.

"I suppose a small look wouldn't be so bad," I thought aloud. My legs started once more towards the window, its light fully enveloping me. Ease seemed to flow through me as the warmth of the sun brought me closer. My arms slowly raised the window. The sun. The beautiful, life giving sun. Gorgeous, gold yellow pollen seeped through the open window, the window now up to its full height. I took a deep breath in, and all my turmoil washed away.

About the Author

It began with a thought, a small flash of an unnerving scene that he had not seen before. **Alex Oleszkiewicz** had more flashes, ideas for what could be planted themselves in his thoughts. Like the roots of a flower, it began to spread throughout his mind. Characters were made, settings set, and so the sprouts of ideas became tall, blossoming plants. When it was all said and done, those who read it had gotten the same seeds as he had. And so the cycle continues.

Teen Published Finalist

The Other Side of the Oak Tree

Harper Mervau

The air was thick with the scent of mulch and possibility, the kind of Michigan autumn afternoon that promised a final, orange, sun-drenched day before the permanent, shivering gray. Eighth grade was out for recess. Trina watched Axel from beneath the sprawling oak tree that marked the edge of the blacktop. His red t-shirt, a hand-me-down from a sports team he was no longer on, was a vibrant flag against the muted backdrop of the school's tired brick. His laugh, a quick, abrupt sound she had come to recognize and adore, was a rhythm she had secretly practiced in her head for months. She'd planned this moment for weeks, the conversation turning into an effortless, charming confession, the kind she'd read about in dog-eared library books. But now, with the moment at hand, the words felt less like effortless poetry and more like jagged, unpolished stones in her throat.

She had spent too many lunch hours watching him with his friends, a silent observer from the periphery of their bustling circle. She knew he loved old-school video games, that he was surprisingly good at kickball despite his lanky frame, and that he always shared his cheese puffs with his best friend, Mark. These were the small, unimportant details that had woven themselves into the fabric of her crush, making it feel less like a fleeting fancy and more like a carefully constructed masterpiece of secret observation. She was a resident of Kentwood, and the school felt like a small-scale version of the whole state: predictable seasons, familiar faces, and the occasional, unexpected storm. She felt the storm brewing in her own chest.

"Axel?" Her voice was small, barely audible over the squeak of the rusty swings and the distant shouts from the kickball game. He turned, his dark hair falling across his forehead, and his smile, so easily given to others, faltered when he saw the serious expression on her face.

"Hey, Trina. What's up?"

She clutched the hem of her sweatshirt, a cheap, fake thing from the school store. It was gray, blending in perfectly with the November sky and the concrete beneath her feet. "I, um... I have something to tell you."

He leaned against the tree, crossing his arms. He looked so tall, so impossibly at ease, a natural fixture of the landscape. The gnarled bark of the oak was rough against his back, a stark contrast to his smooth, tanned skin. "Okay."

"I really like you," she blurted out, her cheeks instantly burning with a heat that had nothing to do with the lingering sunshine. The words felt clumsy and exposed, a tiny, fragile thing dropped on the hard asphalt for all to see. "Like... more than a friend."

He was quiet for a long moment, the silence exaggerating the frantic, hummingbird beat of her heart. She watched his face, searching for a sign, any hint of a corresponding feeling. His expression was soft, his brow furrowed with a gentle kindness that was worse than any scorn he could have shown her. It was the careful face he made when he didn't want to hurt someone, a familiar look she had seen him give to others over the years.

"Trina, that's... really nice of you to say," he began, his tone a hushed, careful murmur. "But I don't feel that way about you. I just think of you as a friend."

The air felt thin, the smell of mulch suddenly cloying and overwhelming. Her lungs, which had been working so hard to contain her bravery, felt suddenly empty. The world, which a moment ago had been so full of potential, seemed to shrink and recede into the distance. The sounds of the playground faded, replaced by a hollow ringing in her ears. The gentle rejection was a deflating balloon, a silent, unremarkable failure. She managed a weak, "Oh. Okay," and before he could say anything else, she turned and walked away. She didn't run, didn't give in to the desperate impulse to flee. Instead, she walked with a purposeful, dignified slowness, as if the rejection hadn't just hollowed her out and left her standing in the vast, empty space of the playground. She found a quiet bench by the building, near a patch of struggling rose bushes, and sat, watching the last golden light of the afternoon fade.

The next day, the school felt different. The air was colder, the hallways louder and more crowded. Trina kept her head down, a solitary asteroid in the orbit of louder, more confident planets. She avoided the oak tree, circling the perimeter of the blacktop to stay as far away from the spot where her confidence had been so gently and thoroughly crushed. She saw Axel by his locker, laughing with his friends, and felt a familiar, sharp pang, but it was dulled now, a manageable ache that she knew would fade with time.

At recess, she sat alone on the same bench, picking at the peeling green paint. The sun was muted, hidden behind a sky the color of old cement. The sound of approaching footsteps was slow and deliberate, but she didn't look up. She assumed it was a teacher or someone who needed her to move.

"Hey. Is this seat taken?"

A voice she didn't recognize, low and kind, cut through the noise of the playground. She looked up and met the gaze of a boy she'd seen in her science class. He had warm, hazel eyes and a smattering of freckles across his nose that gave his face a boyish, approachable quality. She hadn't noticed him before; he existed in a different, quiet corner of the classroom, just as she did.

"No," she said, her voice a little rusty from disuse.

He sat down, leaving a respectful, comfortable amount of space between them. The metal of the bench was cold against her legs. "I'm Leo."

"Trina."

"I know," he said, and gave a slight, shy smile. "We're in biology together. I see you copying down Mrs. Davison's notes like a maniac every day."

She laughed, a small, surprised sound that felt foreign in her ears. "Guilty."

They fell into an easy, natural conversation, the words flowing between them like a quiet stream. Leo talked about his dog, a rambunctious Labrador named Scout, and a frustrating art class project involving clay that he couldn't quite get right. He was funny and easy to talk to, his words flowing without the nervous, calculated rhythm she had used with Axel. He didn't ask her about her crush or her day; he just talked about his, a simple, genuine exchange that felt more valuable than any grand confession. He didn't seem to notice the sad, gray sweatshirt or her quiet demeanor. He just saw Trina, the girl who sat in the back of biology and took meticulous notes.

When the bell rang, signaling the end of recess, he stood up, dusting off his hands.

"So, I was wondering," he said, stuffing his hands in his pockets, his freckled face flushed with a color that reminded her of the last leaves on the oak tree. "If maybe you'd want to, I don't know... get some ice cream after school sometime?"

The offer was so simple, so direct, and so unexpected that it took her a moment to process. It wasn't a grand gesture, but it was genuine. It was a question posed to her, Trina, not Trina-who-had-a-crush. It was a new beginning, offered without judgment or baggage. She looked at his kind eyes and saw no pretense, no expectation, just a quiet curiosity.

"I'd like that," she said, and a real smile, one that reached her eyes, spread across her face. "Yeah. I'd like that a lot."

That night, she wasn't thinking of the oak tree or the boy who didn't like her back. She was thinking of hazel eyes and freckles, of the easy conversation, and a new kind of possibility that felt warmer, more real. The next day, she didn't just walk to recess. She walked with her head held high, looking for the boy with the shy smile, ready to like him back.

About the Author

Harper Mervau is an eighth grade student at St. Patrick Parnell school and an emerging novel writer. Her writing typically focuses on the natural world and the complexities of growing up in the digital age. When she isn't writing, she enjoys golf and volunteering at school. She dreams of publishing her first full romance drama duology before graduating high school.

Youth Judges' Choice Winner

The Ink and the Pencil
Avery Beard

The small town of Wittenburg, in 1938, was quiet and full of stories. Every morning, Eva Rosenberg, a fourteen-year-old Jewish girl, sat under the chestnut tree she would always sit under, writing poems in a worn-out notebook she's had since she was ten. Her best friend, Hans Schneider, drew beside her, moving his pencil smoothly across the page.

"You draw and I'll write, like always." Eva said grinning. "Someday we'll make a book together."

Hans laughed, "We'll write a book as long as I make the cover. Maybe we'll even become wealthy off of the book and live in that house over there." He pointed using his index finger. The

They'd known each other since they were five. Their friendship was as natural as breathing, they were that connected. Soon their friendship became more, it was their first love, they didn't admit it, though.

But, as the years passed, the world around them began to change.

Hans walked home one day and found his father, Karl Schneider, hanging a red flag with a black swastika on their old, creaky porch. His younger sister, Lina, sat at the kitchen table sewing the same symbol onto a sleeve.

"What are those for?" Hans asked.

His dad looked proud. "For Germany! Hitler is saving our nation. You'll join the Hitler Youth like every other boy in town."

Hans froze. "But... Eva's Jewish."

His dad slammed his fist on the table. "Then she's not your friend anymore. Jews are the problem with this country, even the world."

Han's stomach churned. Eva–kind, brave, Eva-wasn't the problem.

That night, Hans couldn't sleep. He stared at the ceiling, then picked up his pencil and began to draw her face.

As Hans drew, he remembered when he and Eva were eight, sitting under the chestnut tree. She had said, "My mom says people fear what they don't understand. So we should always try to understand people."

Back then, he thought it was just something adults said. But now, in a world full of shouting and hate, those words felt like light in the dark.

Over the next few months, Wittenburg changed. Red flags hung from every building. People stopped smiling at Eva's family. A yellow Star of David appeared on their door.

But Hans and Eva still met secretly under the old chestnut tree.

"Promise me something," Eva said one afternoon. "If they take us away, don't forget me."

Hans swallowed hard. "I couldn't, even if I tried."

That night, Hans sat by his window. Should I obey my family and the Nazis? Or should I do what I know is right? What if I get caught? What if I can't help her?

A week later, soldiers came to town. The Rosenbergs were forced from their home. Eva's notebook fell to the ground as she was pushed into a truck.

Hans ran into the street, "Eva!"

She looked back once and mouthed, Don't forget me.

Then she was gone.

Hans went to the chestnut tree every day after that. He lifted a little stone by the trunk and hid small drawings underneath–birds, stars, hearts, and sometimes just her name. He did it over and over again.

Eva and her family were packed into a train car and taken to The concentration camp Auschwitz. The sign above the entrance read, "Arbeit Macht Frei" which means "Work liberates" In German.

Her mother held her hand tightly. "Stay strong, Eva. Stay hopeful."

They entered a line in which their names were replaced by numbers, their hair was shaved off, and they were given striped uniforms.

Even though they were at a concentration camp, Eva refused to stop writing. Whenever she found scrap paper, she scribbled poems and hid them under the floorboards.

At night, she whispered the verses to women around her:

"When all the world forgets my name, the wind will whisper it just the same."

The words gave all the women in their barrack comfort.

One night, as she worked near the fence, a small folded paper fluttered down. Inside was a dove, with her name written under it.

Eva's hand shook. "Hans," she whispered."You're alive."

A few nights later, she saw him in the shadows beyond the barbed wire fence. His face was thinner, but it was him.

"I brought you bread," he whispered. "Hold on. The Allies are coming."

Tears streamed down her eyes."You shouldn't be here, Hans! They'll kill you!" Although, she did think that the bread would taste delightful. With the soft, airy taste of the bread, it would remind her of the challah bread her mom would make back in Wittenberg.

Before he could answer, a guard shouted. Dogs barked. Gunfire cracked.

"Run!" Eva cried.

Hans turned and disappeared into the forest. She never saw him again-but she held the dove close and prayed he had survived.

That night, Eva's mom, Ruth, squeezed Eva's hand and whispered, "Even in hate, find a reason to hope. That's how we survive."

After Hans ran away from camp, he didn't stop running. He sprinted through the forest until his lungs burned. He didn't dare go home-his father would turn him in. For days, he slept in barns and ate scraps.

One night, he heard German soldiers talking near a campfire.

"The Americans are advancing," one said. "They're looking for Germans who will help them fight Hitler."

Hans felt a spark of hope. Maybe that's what I can do. Maybe that's how I can fight for Eva.

He walked for weeks, moving west until he crossed into Allied territory. There, he found American soldiers and surrendered.

At first, they didn't trust him. But when he explained-in halting English-that he wanted to fight against the Nazis, they agreed to take him in as a translator.

Hans wore an American uniform, though it never felt quite real. He traveled with their troops, helping liberate towns and villages.

Each night, after the fighting, he took out his sketchbook. He drew Eva's face. He drew doves, stars, and the chestnut tree just like he had before.

He whispered, "I'll find you again."

He saw terrible things-destroyed homes, frightened children-but he also saw people helping each other, sharing bread, and soldiers giving hope. It reminded him why he was fighting.

And every time he thought of quitting, he remembered Eva's words: Don't forget me.

Back in the concentration camp, time felt endless. People around Eva grew weaker everyday. But she kept writing and whispering poems to give others strength.

Then, one spring morning, the sound of gunfire came from beyond the fences. Shouts echoed. Soldiers in green uniforms–Americans–broke through the gates.

"Freedom!" someone cried.

Eva stood frozen. The soldiers were real. They were smiling. Some were even crying.

She stepped outside of the camp for the first time in years and felt the sunlight on her skin. It was warm, bright, and alive.

Eva realized that hope had carried her through the darkest time. Her mother's words, Hans' drawing, her poems–all of it had kept her alive.

Months later, Eva returned home to Wittenburg. The town was quieter, scarred, but still standing. The pavement was cracked, and the chestnut tree had lost some branches.

She sat in her old spot under the tree, softly running her fingers on the old, peeling bark of the tree. Then, she opened a new notebook. Her hand trembled as she began to write:

Ink for memory, pencil for hope, together they tell our story.

Footsteps crunched behind her.

"Still writing, I see," said a familiar voice.

Eva turned, her heart racing. "Hans?"

He was thinner, older, and dressed in a patched-up uniform–but his eyes still held the same light.

"I told you I'd draw the cover," he said, smiling. He lifted up the same sketchbook he used when they were little. In the drawing, Eva and him were sitting by the old tree, as always, she was writing and he was drawing.

Eva threw her arms around him, laughing and crying at the same time. "You came back!"

"So did you," Hans whispered. "You kept hope alive, didn't you?"

Eva nodded. "Just like you told me to."

They sat together again–her pen gliding across the paper, his pencil sketching beside her. The breeze whistled behind them, as if nothing had changed.

A year later, the people of Wittenburg gathered beneath the chestnut tree for their wedding.

The bride, Eva Rosenberg, wore a beautiful white lace dress. And for the groom, Hans Schneider, he wore a gray suit. They were surrounded by townspeople who finally knew what courage looked like.

At the ceremony, Eva read her final poem:

"When hate tried to break us, hope held us fast. The ink and the pencil had joined us at last."

Hans smiled and held up his sketchbook. Inside was one final drawing–two hands, one holding a pen, the other a pencil, joined in the middle of a heart.

They lived their life happily, dwelling in the light blue house they had both admired, and eventually published the book they made together.

About the Author

Avery Beard is a young writer who enjoys telling meaningful stories inspired by history and real-life struggles. She has been interested in historical fiction since she was young and believes that hope is crucial during the trials of life. Avery wants readers to be informed about the past and understand why remembering history matters. As Holocaust survivor Elie Wiesel said, "For the dead and the living, we must bear witness," a quote that reflects her belief that telling stories about the past helps honor those who suffered and ensures we learn from history. Through her stories, she aims to show that kindness, courage, and hope can exist even in darkest of times.

Youth Judges' Choice Runner-Up
Olive and Her Magical Cotton Candy
Olive Davis

Olive was a little girl with big, curious eyes, a mischievous smile, and a heart full of wonder. She loved to play tricks, climb trees when she wasn't supposed to, and sometimes sneak cookies before dinner. At school, Olive sometimes got into trouble for chatting too much or making funny faces in class, but she always managed to get good grades, surprising her teachers and her mom alike.

Her best friend was Jakeera. They shared everything — secrets, jokes, and the occasional silly prank. Jakeera loved adventures as much as Olive did, and together, they made a great team.

Olive's mom, Jalita, was a loving woman who cared deeply about her daughter. Jalita wanted Olive to grow up healthy and strong, which meant watching what Olive ate — especially when it came to sweets like cotton candy.

"Too much sugar isn't good for you, Olive," Jalita would say gently, shaking her head. "Cotton candy is just sugar spun around a stick. It won't keep you healthy or strong."

Olive understood, but it made her heart ache a little. She wished she could enjoy her favorite treat without worrying about getting in trouble.

One Monday morning, Olive sat at her desk, trying hard to pay attention to her math lesson. But Jakeera, sitting next to her, made a silly face that made Olive giggle. The teacher caught her whispering and gave a polite warning.

"Olive, remember to focus, please," the teacher said kindly.

Olive nodded, but inside she was already thinking of their next plan for recess — maybe a game of tag or a secret handshake.

At recess, Olive and Jakeera found a quiet spot behind the big oak tree. "I bet you can't catch me!" Olive teased, dashing away with a playful grin.

Jakeera laughed and chased after her, their laughter echoing across the playground.

Despite her mischievous side, Olive was proud of her good grades. Her teachers often complimented her on her bright ideas and quick thinking.

One bright Saturday morning, the town's annual fair came to life with colorful banners, laughing children, and delicious smells floating in the air. Olive's family walked hand in hand through the bustling crowd. And there it was — the cotton candy stand, brighter and bigger than ever.

Olive's eyes went wide. She tugged on Jalita's sleeve, whispering, "Can I please have some cotton candy? Just a little bit?"

Jalita looked down and smiled softly but shook her head. "Maybe just this once, Olive, but only a small bite. And you have to promise me you'll brush your teeth afterward."

Olive nodded eagerly, barely able to contain her excitement.

With a quick shuffle of coins, the cotton candy vendor handed Olive a fluffy pink cloud wrapped carefully around a stick. Olive held it carefully, feeling like she had just caught a fairy's secret.

She took a small bite, and the sugary fluff melted instantly on her tongue, sweet and soft like a dream. She savored every little bit, careful not to eat too much.

Suddenly, a gentle breeze swept through the fair, and something magical happened.

The cotton candy started to glow — first a soft pink light, then sparkling sparkles danced around it like tiny stars. Olive blinked, amazed. The cotton candy wasn't just a treat — it was alive with magic!

"Hello, Olive," a tiny voice whispered from the sugary cloud. "I'm Candy, the Cotton Candy Fairy."

Olive's eyes grew even bigger. "A fairy? Really?"

"Yes," Candy said with a giggle. "I'm here to remind you that a little sweetness in life is okay, but balance is the true magic."

Olive thought about Jalita's words. "So... I can enjoy cotton candy sometimes, but I need to be careful?"

Candy nodded. "Exactly! And I'll help you remember the magic of balance — so you can have fun without any worries."

From that day on, Olive and Candy became the best of friends. Whenever Olive felt the urge for cotton candy, Candy would appear, sparkling and cheerful, reminding her to enjoy just a little bit — and to take care of herself too.

Jalita noticed the change. She saw Olive brushing her teeth diligently and choosing healthy snacks along with her occasional cotton candy treats. Even though Olive could be a little mischievous at times — at school or at home — her good grades and growing sense of responsibility made Jalita proud.

A few weeks later, Olive felt something wiggly in her mouth. Her front tooth was loose! She was excited but also a little nervous.

"Mom, my tooth is moving!" Olive said, wiggling it with her tongue. Jalita leaned over and smiled warmly. "Looks like someone's about to lose their first tooth!"

Olive jumped up and down, her eyes wide with excitement. "Do you think I'll get a gold coin? Or maybe a sparkly fairy note?"

Jalita chuckled. "You'll have to wait and see. But remember, the Tooth Fairy only visits when the tooth is clean and under your pillow."

"I'll brush it five times!" Olive shouted, already sprinting to the bathroom.

That night, Olive brushed her teeth like a superhero. First up, down, then side to side — and don't forget the tongue! When she finally climbed into bed, she carefully placed her tiny tooth in a purple jewelry box and tucked it under her pillow.

She whispered, "Candy... if you see the Tooth Fairy, tell her hi from me!"

As the stars twinkled outside her window, Olive drifted off to sleep. But something amazing happened while she snored softly in her blanket burrito.

A swirl of glitter sparkled in the room — and pop! Candy the Cotton Candy Fairy floated down from the ceiling, glowing softly. Beside her fluttered a second fairy, wearing a sparkly dress made of moonlight and silver shoes.

"Hi, Candy," the second fairy whispered. "This must be Olive's room."

"She's been very good," Candy said proudly. "Even chose an apple instead of cookies yesterday!"

Twinkle, the Tooth Fairy, giggled. "I love to see that! Let's leave her something special."

They hovered over the pillow, lifting it gently with magic sparkles. Twinkle placed a shiny coin wrapped in a tiny note:

Dear Olive,

You're doing a wonderful job taking care of your smile! Keep brushing, keep laughing, and remember — a little sweetness is okay when your heart is big and your habits are strong.

Shine on!

— Twinkle

Candy added a tiny cotton candy-shaped charm, one that smelled like strawberries and magic.

Then, with a swirl of sparkles and a quiet whoosh, the two fairies disappeared into the night sky.

The next morning, Olive woke up and dove under her pillow.

"Jakeera's never gonna believe this!" she shouted. "I got a note, a coin, and a charm!"

She ran into the kitchen, waving the goodies in the air. Jalita raised her eyebrows. "Wow, looks like the Tooth Fairy thinks you're extra special."

"She does! And Candy came too — I know it!"

That day at school, Olive showed Jakeera the charm and the note. "I think the fairies are working together," she whispered. "Maybe they're part of a secret fairy club."

Jakeera grinned. "Can I join?"

"Of course," Olive said. "But you have to brush your teeth and eat your veggies."

Jakeera groaned. "Even the green ones?"

Olive nodded. "Especially the green ones. Candy says balance is the real magic."

And from that day on, the two friends made a fairy club of their own — full of giggles, kindness, sparkles... and just a little bit of cotton candy.

About the Author

Olive Davis is the 2025-2026 Write Michigan Short Story Contest Judges' Choice Runner-Up winner in the Youth category.

Youth Readers' Choice Winner

The Creature, the Magician, and the Cabin
Delilah Nicholl

Prologue

"Come on, Emily, we've got to go!" yelled my older brother James.

"Coming!" yelled Emily.

Emily took one last look at the old house she had lived in her whole life, the small house in North Carolina where all her best memories were made. Tears welled in her eyes; she took one final glance and trudged out the door.

Chapter 1

It was a long drive to the new house in Tennessee, and Emily's littlest sister, Luna, wouldn't stop asking,

"Are we there yet?" But everyone ignored her.

It took four and a half hours to get there. When they finally arrived, her younger brother, Asher, jumped out of the car and started running laps around the new driveway while Violet, her little sister, refused to get out of the car because she didn't want to move. Emily studied the area. The house was cloaked by a large expanse of trees topped with the remaining burnt orange leaves of autumn, mountains peeking out from behind them in the distance.

When they got inside the new house, they all started claiming rooms. Asher and James shared the biggest room, and Luna, Emily, and Violet all got their own mid-sized room, each with a bathroom and a window seat overlooking the Smoky Mountains outside. Emily brought her bags into her room to start unpacking. When she finished, she asked her mother if she could go outside to explore. She said yes, and so she set out into the woods to adventure.

Deep in the woods, she found a cabin.

"What's this?" Emily said to herself. As she got nearer, she saw that the cabin was very old. Warily, she walked over to it and turned the doorknob; it opened easily, and she walked inside.

Chapter 2

Inside, she saw the most peculiar thing. What should have been the inside of a cabin was a spinning portal covering the walls; it was every color you could have imagined, with thousands of creatures she had never seen before. Lions with wings of an eagle, humans with goat legs, which Emily recalled from Greek mythology were called Satyrs, and other odd creatures, more than you could count! Emily turned back to find that the door had vanished, and she was trapped in this vortex. She spotted a creature staring at her. She cautiously approached it.

"Excuse me? Where am I?" She asked.

"Why, you're in the solar stream of course!" exclaimed the creature.

"The solar stream?" "What's that?" Emily asked.

"Well, you see, the solar stream is a portal we use to travel to different worlds." Said the creature.

"Tell me, what is your name?" The creature asked.

"I-I'm Emily," "Who are y-you?" She stuttered, hands trembling.

"My name is Atlas." Replied the creature.

"Not to b-be rude, b-but what exactly are y-you?" Emily asked. "I'm a Creatarous,

A Creatarous had the wings of an eagle, a lion's body and paws, and a head of a human.

"Come, I will take you to Mythentia and show you around." Said Atlas.

In the blink of an eye, they had warped into Mythentia. It was beautiful. The air was sweet, there were butterflies fluttering around, which were twice the size of the ones on Earth, the statues displayed amongst the vast variety of flowers were incredible, and every creature went about in peace. It was like a dream to be in Mythentia. Atlas motioned for Emily to hop onto her back. Once she had mounted Atlas, they flew over Mythentia. Emily saw the most beautiful sights, like mountains with Satyrs carved in the side, a bay shaped like a Minotaur, and plains speckled with tranquil centaurs roaming about.

"Atlas?" Asked Emily. "This has really been quite enjoyable, but I'd best be getting back home now."

"But you haven't even met the Mythentians yet." Said Atlas.

"The Mythentians? Who are they?" Emily asked.

"Why, they rule Mythentia of course!" "They have unbelievable powers."

"Well, I guess I could stay a little longer." Said Emily, and they set off to meet the Mythentians.

Chapter 3

As Emily grew closer to the Mythentians' palace, she was bewildered.

Imagine the White House merged with the Taj Mahal, then imagine it eight times bigger, made of pure marble, and then you have the Mythentians Palace. Once they landed, Emily jumped off of Atlas's back and ran up to the marble doors of the palace, bewildered.

"Can we go inside?" Emily asked hopefully.

"Yes, but just for a little while," said Atlas. Emily was stunned as she walked into the palace; she had to pinch herself to make sure she wasn't dreaming.

"This way to the Mythentian's quarters," Atlas said.

As they walked down a long, dim hallway, Emily got the feeling she was being watched.

"Atlas?" "I really should be getting back now," Emily said.

"NO!" Atlas roared. She whirled around to face Emily. She looked nothing like she had before; the once beautiful creatarous now looked like a demon, her eyes were glowing red, her lion's claws were extended, she was reared up on her hind legs, and she bared her fangs, sharp as a knife, ready to bite. But the weirdest thing was that no light whatsoever touched her; she was enshrouded by shadows. She spoke in a voice that was nothing like before. It was deep and full of anger. Emily started to slowly back away until she felt a cold marble wall on her back. Atlas approached Emily until she was cornered. Emily heard the roar of a lion, then felt a huge paw slam her head into the wall very hard. She screamed so loud she almost shattered the glass windows, and then everything went black.

Chapter 4

Emily awoke to see nothing but never-ending darkness surrounding her. The world around her was gone. Am I dead? Emily thought.

"Hello?" Emily asked the darkness. No response.

Emily tried to walk into the darkness, but as she did, the darkness seemed to grow.

"The further you walk, the bigger it gets," said an eerie voice.

"Who's there? Stay away from me!" Emily squeaked.

"I am the magician." The voice returned.

Out of the corner of her eye, Emily saw a shadow dash behind her.

"What's happening? Where am I?" Emily asked.

"Well, let me start from the beginning. You see, a long time ago, Atlas was very jealous of the Mythentians. She thought that if she could get rid of them, she could rule Mythentia. So she gathered many other followers to help her, and with their help, she trapped the Mythenians and forced them through the Solar stream to Tartarus, a dark prison in which you can not escape. So then, to this day, the few of us who still support the Mythentians are in hiding. Lately, Atlas has been going to Earth to set up traps disguised as things humans will find intriguing, and venture into, then she waits in the solar stream to find them and lure them in, she takes them to Mythentia and befriends them. Then, she attacks them once they let their guard down and traps them in here for me to turn them to stone, and then you get put in her statue garden outside the palace. But if you get lucky, she'll make you her slave. Though I haven't turned anyone to stone in ages, mainly because no one has gotten trapped for years, until today."

"Please don't turn me to stone! I just want to get home!" She pleaded with the Magician.

"Relax, young child, I am done helping that beast. You need to get out of here. Go deep into your mind and think of the place you want to go."

"Thank you." She said, relieved.

Emily thought as hard as she could to be right outside the cabin that led to the portal.

Chapter 5

Emily felt light as a feather as she slipped through the solar stream back to earth.

"Ouch!"

She felt hard ground on her spine. She stood up, looked over her shoulder, and saw her house.

"Emily, dinner!" She heard her mom yell.

"Coming!" Emily called back, and she ran back to the house.

As she sat down to eat dinner, her mother asked...

"Did you find anything good?"

"Yeah," she casually replied. And so she told her family all about her long adventure in Mythentia, about Atlas and the magician, and the beautiful world within the solar stream, knowing very well that no one would believe her, but she was fine with that. It could be her special secret.

About the Author

Delilah Nicholl is an avid reader of all genres, her favorites being fantasy and adventure. She loves being outdoors and going on hikes in the woods, where she daydreams and pictures herself in her favorite stories. She loves playing piano and violin and likes to write her own music. She lives in Grosse Pointe Woods with her parents and her beloved old dog, Mabel.

Youth Published Finalist

Just Try
Juliet Einfeld

Thump! I set down my suitcase in the doorway, taking a long look at the house where I would be living in for the next...who knows how long?

It was a gloomy day in November—you know, the typical drizzly kind? Anyway, my dad and I just moved to Edinburgh, Scotland because of my dad's stupid social media work. He really wanted to start over and post in Scotland because that's apparently where all the famous influencers post. That's where all the buzz is. Annoying, right? I had an almost perfect life before the move. Before we moved to Scotland, we lived in the United States. But ever since my mom died of cancer, he couldn't take it anymore, so we moved here.

I can still remember my beautiful mother, before cancer robbed her away from me and Dad. I can still remember her sweet gaze every time I would tell her a story about school. Or when she would explain something to me whenever there was something in a story that I didn't understand. I can remember one moment in particular, it's still as clear as day:

I must have been about four years old, my mom and I were reading a story. It was about a gingerbread man that lived in a beautiful kingdom of gingerbread people.

"Mama, what is gingerbread?"

"Honey, gingerbread is like a graham cracker that tastes sweet and spicy. It's really yummy. Remember when I got you that special snack for your birthday that you really liked?"

"Yes, Mama."

"That's gingerbread. And remember when we decorate little houses for Christmas that you can eat? It is made of gingerbread."

"Mmm, you're making me hungry, Mama."

She laughed, it was a beautiful sound, like birds on a bright and sunny morning.

Oh, Mama.

Now, Dad and I live alone. I don't know why I was the one who had to be dragged halfway across the world for some dumb project.

Now there's a new school. New people. Practically an entirely new life. So far, it's as miserable as a raccoon digging in a trash bin, hoping for something superb but coming back out with nothing but a cheese stick wrapper.

I looked around. The house was furnished. In the living room, the furniture looked lumpy and the coffee table looked worn. I looked up to see a dimly lit chandelier, missing a few glass crystals.

I sighed. Everything just felt...wrong. It was too dark and there was a musty smell that needed to go.

The dark wooden floorboards creaked under my feet as I crossed the compact house to a small window on the other side of the living room. I opened up the window and took a long sniff of the air outside. Leaving the window open I headed to the stairs. I counted them as I climbed up.

"One...two...three..." and so on. When I reached the top, I had counted twenty stairs. I stared at the narrow hallway before me, it had pale green walls with a few paintings. One was a picture of a man playing the bagpipe, a traditional Scottish instrument. I'd tried it before at school when a musical group visited to show our class back in second grade. It's definitely not as easy as it looks.

Creak! The door to my new bedroom opened up to reveal a cramped little bedroom with a small twin sized bed in one corner. It had a soft cream colored blanket and puffy pillows. At least the bed looked comfortable. There was a closet in another and a large dresser that looked out of place in the tightly packed bedroom. "Well, it's not as bad as it could be." I muttered to myself.

***

The next morning was school. Boring and dull as it was in the US, maybe it will be different here. I quickly ate a breakfast of leftover takeout that we got the night before.

"I'm going to school now!" I yelled at Dad.

"Mmh," He responded. I rolled my eyes. He was already on his many computers, which he was on every day from seven in the morning to six at night.

I took that as an 'ok' and headed off toward school, only a couple blocks away. I stared at my shoes as I walked down the street.

"Oof!" A pinch of pain shot up my arm as I fell on the pavement in front of the school. "Arrgh," I grumbled as I rubbed my elbow. I looked around, a girl with ginger hair laying on the ground in front of me was wearing the same uniform as me: a scratchy plaid skirt and an itchy cardigan sweater.

"Sorry!" I exclaimed. "I wasn't watching where I was going."

"It's all right! You're just being a little numptie!" The girl said as if the crash hadn't even happened. I wasn't sure if being called 'numptie' was something good, but it didn't sound bad. "I wasn't either." She had a thick Scottish accent, "My name is Blair," she said, extending her hand.

"I'm Mae," I said, taking her hand and shaking it.

"You're American!"

"Yeah, I'm new here, first day at school and all." I explained uncomfortably. We both got up.

"Buzzin'!" Blair said cheerfully, "I can show you around! Can I see your schedule?"

 I took out my schedule and handed it to her.

"Smashin'! We have the same classes!" She handed back my schedule. "Come on, I'll take you around."

***

"I'm home!" I said to the almost-empty house. There was no answer. I rolled my eyes and headed toward the kitchen to get a snack. I opened the fridge just to see…nothing, nothing and more nothing. Ugh. Looks like we need more food.

"Yeah, there's no more food left Mae," Dad said, as if he had read my mind. "You could maybe go to the store?" Dad's eyes were still glued to his screens.

"I guess." I said, so I set off to the closest supermarket.

 I scanned the shelves searching for at least something familiar. I looked down aisle seven, Pasta! I will make pasta tonight, I promised myself. I grabbed it and went to the check out.

"Is this all?" Said the cashier in monotone. Unlike Blair, she was as captivating as a blank screen, as exciting as watching grass grow, as lifeless as a stuffed shirt. I could go on and on. I stared at her. But everyone knows that time doesn't wait for anyone.

"Yes." I said tentatively as if I were scared that if I said anything too exciting she might kick me out of the store.

"That will be three pound sterlings, Miss." I really doubt that she had anything exciting happen to her in the last, oh I don't know, maybe two decades? But anyway, I grabbed the money out of my pocket and handed it to the tiresome cashier.

"Thank you!" I said cheerfully, trying to lift her mood, but to no avail, it didn't do anything to lighten her spirit. Let alone wipe that terrible scowl right off her face.

The cashier didn't say anything, so I just left. As I was walking home, I saw someone familiar, I squinted, trying to make out who it was...Blair! That's who it was, at least I think. She was standing on the steps of a house that I assumed was hers.

"Mae, isn't it?" Yelled someone. It was Blair.

"Yeah!" I said, trying to match her enthusiasm.

"I would like to invite you to my house for dinner tomorrow night!" She said excitedly as soon as she got close enough to not have to yell.

"Great! That sounds like so much fun, I'll be planning on it." I said, assuming Dad wouldn't care.

"Okay! See you there!" Then, she said to me, "It's the house we're standing in front of."

I nodded, then she left. I watched her skip away and then went home myself.

***

"I'm going to Blair's house now!" I yelled at Dad.

"Mkay," he responded.

I turned around, closed the door and started toward Blair's house.

When I got there, Blair was waiting for me on the front porch, drawing in a little red sketchbook.

"Hi!" She said, when she saw me. I waved, smiling. "I've been planning out our evening together." Instead of sketching, she was making a list of things that we were to do. It looked like this:

Fun things to do with Mae!!!!!!!

Dinner!

Dessert!

Games!

Even what she wrote had to end with an exclamation mark.

"Cool," I said.

"Come on, let's go inside before the food gets cold!" declared Blair. "Oh! First, we need to take a selfie!" Blair whipped out her phone and snapped a quick photo. "There! Now everyone can know how smashin' tonight is gonna be!" I assumed that meant that she posted on social media. Maybe my dad would see it.

"Can we eat now? I'm so hungry I could eat ten silver eagles!" I said.

"Golden eagles." Blair corrected.

"Oh." I said, embarrassed. "Isn't the Golden eagle the bird for Scotland?"

"Yes! They really are magnificent."

We walked up the stone steps to her house, the door was dark and walnut colored with a tiny window at the top. The door creaked as we stepped inside. It was very welcoming. Cozy chairs sat by the roaring fire in the fireplace.

"Welcome!" Said a woman in the front entrance. She had strawberry blonde hair and a warm gaze that made me feel right at home.

"Thank you, your house is beautiful." I replied.

"Oh, why thank you, you can call me Mrs. Campbell if you'd like." Mrs. Campbell said, flattered. "Blair, love, why don't you head to the kitchen with your friend and I'll have dinner ready in a few minutes?"

"Okay! Come on, you have to try my mother's fish and chips."

We sat down at the table as Mrs. Campbell put the plate full of fish and chips in front of me. I tried not to let the smell get in the way of being polite. My hands started to sweat, I closed my eyes and—

Crunch.

The flaky crust of the fish dissolved in my mouth and the buttery, soft fish slipped down my throat in a surprisingly satisfying way. My eyes lit up.

This. Is. Amazing. I thought.

Blair giggled. "Never had fish before? It's amazing, right?"

I nodded enthusiastically, my mouth too full of deliciousness to say anything.

"Okay just one more photo," said Blair. She posted the next photo and I caught a glimpse of it and it was called: #BestNightEver!!!

We finished up the delicious fish and chips and Blair said that I had to have dessert.

"What's for dessert?" I asked.

"We're having...Dundee cake!" She said very excitedly, "It's so good"

"Okay! Just one question, what is it?"

"That." She pointed to a large circular bread loaf that had sugar and almonds on top with a little bowl of marmalade on the side to spread on your cake. To be totally honest it looked and smelled amazing.

Mrs. Campbell cut me a large slice of cake and handed it to me with a little bowl of marmalade. "Please, eat as much as you want, there's plenty!"

I closed my eyes and bit into it. I gasped; my eyes popped open. My taste buds applauded. "What is in this?! It's amazing!"

"I know, right? My mom makes the best Dundee cake."

Maybe life wouldn't be so bad after all. Mrs. Campbell's cooking was exquisite.

Bzzzt.

Blair's phone buzzed. She glanced at it. Then, she showed it to me, one of the comments on Blair's latest post read:

#IsThatMyDaughter?!

"Yup. That's Dad." I said disappointedly, "I should probably get home now, make sure Dad isn't too worried. He probably didn't even know I left. That's why he sounded so surprised." I suppressed a heavy sigh.

"Okay, well, we didn't get to the games, but you can come over tomorrow again if you want!" Said Blair, eagerly.

I nodded, then I grabbed my jacket and hat and slipped out the door before they could see the growing tears in my eyes.

***

"Why didn't you tell me you were leaving!" Dad roared. "I was worried, you could have gotten lost, or kidnapped!"

I scoffed, "hard to believe you're worried about someone who's not yourself."

"Of course I was worried about you. You're my daughter!" He cried.

"Believe what you want, I told you I was leaving!" My anger started to escalate, leading to my voice getting hoarse from yelling at Dad.

"Well," he huffed hotly, "I don't remember that!"

"Well of course you don't, you don't remember anything but your own accomplishments on your stupid social media!" At that point, my fists were clenched and tears began to roll down my cheeks. I turned on my heel and stomped to the creaky old stairs. I made my footsteps as loud as I could just to annoy my dad.

Then, I opened my bedroom door and slammed it hard after me. I bet if I slammed it any harder, it would be blown off its hinges.

I angrily laid down on my bed and cried myself to sleep.

***

Days passed, maybe weeks. But I felt trapped in my own misery. Like rain. When Blair invited me over, I would say: 'Maybe another time. Thanks for offering though.' And when Dad tried to talk to me, I would ignore him and walk away pretending not to hear him. Every day, I wake up, eat, school, dinner, and sleep. The process just repeats itself. Over and over.

***

Finally, it was Saturday morning—again. I rubbed my puffy red eyes and went into the bathroom to get ready. I looked in the mirror and to my horror, my hair looked as if a squirrel tried to style it while I slept. It was sticking out unnaturally in some places and so knotted in others that it looked like it should probably have just been cut off to save me from the hassle instead of just brushing it out.

I groaned. This was going to take a while. So I painfully brushed it out as I winced, cringed, yelped, grimaced and flinched. What did I do during the night, gymnastics?

I finally finished and my hair and it ended up being puffy and voluminous, maybe a little too voluminous. It'll have to do because I was hoping not to be out of the house and instead just sit around and read. But other things stopped me from that…

"Mae, I need to show you something!" Dad called from downstairs, why wasn't he in his study? I could tell that his voice was not coming from his office.

"Not now, Dad," I told him, remembering last night.

"Please, it'll just take a second, and I think you're gonna like it."

"Fine." I said. I walked down stairs to find an awful smell. Dad must be trying to cook. I concluded. I remember that he had tried to do this before Mom passed away but stopped after she wasn't there anymore to encourage him to get better.

I almost headed straight out the door, but I was still in my pajamas and I at least wanted to see what he was trying to cook.

I stumbled into the kitchen and the smell was even more sickening than before.

"Why?" I griped.

"Why what?" Dad asked, a little angry at my rotten attitude.

"Why must you try to start cooking again? We were better off ordering take out every day!"

"Because I wanted to surprise you. You should be grateful that you don't have to make breakfast for yourself anymore, I'm doing it every morning from now on!" He said, a smile surfacing on his face.

"Don't you have something better to do?" I asked, the bitterness still managed to seep into my tone of voice.

"Nope! I put a time limit on myself for my work time, so now we can do something together,"

"Who are you and what have you done with my dad?" I asked suspiciously, squinting my eyes at him. What in the world happened to him? I wondered.

"What do you mean?" He questioned.

"In the past couple of weeks, you were this crazy social media enthusiast and now you're...nice?" The words felt wrong on my tongue.

Dad sighed as he leaned on the counter. "Listen, I know I've been a little—"

"Overbearing? Inconsiderate?" I interrupted.

"Yes, but I want to make it up to you, that's why I made some changes to my schedule. Over the past few days, I realized...that you were right. I have been a bit distant. And, I'm really sorry."

We sat in silence.

I looked down at my sockless feet. Was Dad right? Did we need to just say sorry and move on? I feel like it would be so hard to do. To live with someone who has been aloof for most of my life? I don't know...

More silence. I finally looked up, Dad looked concerned.

I sighed heavily, I've made up my decision. "I'm sorry too." I said. "I have been kinda mean to you, and I really am sorry."

Dad crossed the kitchen toward me to lead me to sit at the counter. I looked at the plate that lay distressingly in front of me with burnt pancakes and charred hashbrowns.

Dad chuckled, it really was a joyful sound. "You don't have to eat that, you know."

"Believe me, I know." I smiled back. Then, something miraculous happened; He opened his arms and I sank into them. He was warm and strong but also gentle at the same time.

I think we could make this work. I thought.

We parted and I swear that our smiles were miles wide.

"I promise to try, at least try to make things as best we can in between us." I declared.

"I promise if you promise," Dad said.

"I promise."

About the Author

Juliet Einfeld is a sixth grader who loves creative activities such as art, writing, cooking and so much more! She lives right down the street from her cousins and participates in many hilarious shenanigans with them. She loves snuggling with her dog Seymour and enjoys spending time with her family and friends.

Youth Published Finalist

The Oasis
Evan Kaltz

From the very beginning, everyone knew that Galaen was different. He was the only Neuborn in the birth chamber who didn't scream like a broken computer, and by the time he was three, he had mastered the art of escape, chasing the FeLinear around his home cubicle until his distraught parents scooped him back into his crib. By the time he was seven, he had advanced to the highest rank in competitive holochess.

However, there was one thing Galaen did not show prowess at from an early age: school. Try as he might, he was unable to process the cold, strict AIschool Programs and the seemingly thousands of rules they created. As the years progressed, so too did the amount of disappointed looks from his parents and warnings from his classes' Programs.

"What I don't get," he confessed to the FeLinear one evening in third grade, " is why they punish us for being normal kids. Today the History Program told me off for 'lack of attention." I mean, sure I was daydreaming, but I'd already read today's chapter!"

The FeLinear stared at him apathetically and flicked its robotic tail. Galaen stared mournfully at the little bot. "It's okay, I don't expect you to understand," he muttered. But all the same, he wished he had someone to confess his feelings to.

One particularly bland day when Galaen was twelve, he got his wish.

As he was riding his electrocycle back from school, grumbling about the atrocities he had been subjected to that day, he noticed a small sign. It was sticking out from between the darkly hued, cluttered cubicles and shops like a tiny computer chip in a wastebin. It had unintelligible words on it, and Galaen was sure he'd never seen it before. He decided to investigate, since he didn't have to be back until dinner and had nothing better to do.

He entered the lift to the higher levels, but by the time he'd ascended to the sign's height, its meaning was clear. A scientific study about (according to the sign) Neurological Decline in Anthropomorphs of Terraceous

Descent was taking place in the shop. Galaen couldn't help but wonder what the almost foreign words meant.

"Hello?" he called, pedaling up to the storefront window. There was no response, so he peered in. Nothing.

Frustrated, Galaen tried the door, and it opened with a hiss. He stepped cautiously inside. The small front room was dark and apparently deserted, with little furnishings other than a metal desk and scattered tools. However, a small light shone from underneath an antique wooden door on the far side of the room.

"Is anyone there?" he asked loudly, then realized a second too late that this was the worst possible thing he could have done. Now whoever it was through that door would catch him for sure. He quickly turned to leave — and collided straight into somebody.

Both Galaen and the stranger tumbled to the floor. "Oi!" the stranger bellowed. "Whaddya think you're doing?"

"I'm not the one screaming their lungs out," Galaen replied. The stranger's glare softened, and they seemed to flash a bright smile in the dusky room.

"I'm Rona," the stranger said. "It's nice to meetcha." She was young - a little older than Galaen - and sporting chestnut brown hair and deep green eyes.

"What are you doing here?" Galaen asked.

"Same reason you are — snooping," said Rona. "The techies down there-" here she pointed to the door, "are up to no good. Ya know what? It'd be easier if I just show ya."

Rona got up and opened the door, which made a muffled noise. Galaen glanced at the hinges and saw a sort of putty covering them. Rona winked. "Masking sealant. One of my specialties."

They crept down a narrow hallway, lit only by a penlight on the ground, which Rona picked up. "Dropped it when I heard ya coming," she explained.

They reached a modern, metal door, which Rona opened with some caution. Galaen's eyes were flooded with bright light, and he glanced around, looking for the source. The entire room, or at least the part that Galaen could see, was filled with barred metal cages. Each cage had a light of varying size and one AnimaTron of each different type and size.

Or at least, Galaen thought they were AnimaTrons. As he looked closer, he saw that no part of them looked robotic; the fur wasn't 3D printed and the eyes weren't minicams, not to mention the fact that they were behaving abnormally for usually emotionless robots. The non-Trons were thrashing violently in the tiny spaces allowed to them, obviously in pain.

Galaen reeled back, horrified. What horrors were going on in this subterranean torture chamber? He turned to Rona, expecting to see an anguished expression on her face as there certainly was on his, but she strode between the cages, showing nothing but raw determination. She beckoned for him to follow and, when he didn't, turned confusedly. Upon seeing him, she quickly donned an obviously false grimace. "Awful, ain't it?"

"Shut up!" screamed Galaen. "You're trying to use me for something and I know it! Why don't you just go... blow something up! Or... something," he finished lamely. As soon as he said it, he regretted the harsh words. The room was slowly driving him insane, he realized, and he had let it get the better of him.

"Geez," said Rona with a hint of cold fury beneath her calm words. "Sorry I bothered." And she turned around and disappeared into the unknown expanse beyond the cages.

Galaen sank down between the metal bars. Hot tears welled up in his eyes, and he blinked furiously, trying to rid himself of their prickly feeling. He wished he was in his home cubicle with his parents, blissfully unaware of the terrors in this evil room.

Suddenly, Galaen felt something familiarly soft brush against his arm. He whipped around, expecting to see his old FeLinear, broken three years but somehow come to comfort him from beyond the grave. But instead, he laid eyes upon a caged non-Tron that looked remarkably like his dead model. Its deep green eyes soothed him, and his body relaxed. But a second later, he sprang up again. "I've got to find a way to free you! I can't let you just die here, after all!"

However, as soon as Galaen said it, he realized that he had no idea how to do this. He would need the help of an expert.

"Wait. An expert..." he muttered. The non-Linear gave him an annoyed look, as if it was irritated that he hadn't figured it out. Galaen racked his mind, thinking about the problem. What did the nonLinear expect him to do?

Suddenly, remembering the masking sealant and the unlocked door, he understood. "Rona."

***

Galaen raced through the rows of cages. "Rona! Where are you?" he called, without success. She was nowhere to be found.

Suddenly, Galaen noticed a small light. A penlight... "Rona!" he yelled, catching sight of her chestnut hair. "Rona, I..."

Without warning, she turned around and slapped him. "Shuttit, ya little glitch!" Galaen was taken aback by her rude words.

"Rona, I'm sorry. I didn't mean what I said earlier. I want to help you!" He looked at her pleadingly.

"I told you to shut it!" Rona was close to tears; her eyes were moist and her voice quivered. She turned to run, but Galaen grabbed her arm.

"Rona, I'm sorry! I didn't mean to hurt your feelings, I didn't mean any of the things I said, and I definitely didn't mean to imply anything about you! I... I wish I could take it all back."

"Well, ya can't, can you?" asked Rona. But her eyes twinkled and, unable to stop it, she smiled. "Whaddya want me to do? Blow th' cages up?"

"I was thinking more along the lines of picking the locks," Galaen replied. "But blowing them up would work too." She punched him. "Okay, okay! Sorry."

"You'd better be," Rona warned teasingly. "But seriously. Which cage should I open first?"

"I'll show you," said Galaen, relieved that Rona had forgiven him. They crept through the narrow spaces between cages until they reached the cage that contained the non-Linear. Rona fiddled with the lock for a short time until it popped open with a snap. The nonLinear dashed out and wound itself gratefully around Rona's legs.

"This 'un's kinda cute," Rona admitted. A smile stretched into existence across her face, and Galaen noticed for the first time how pretty she looked when she was happy. "Now," said Rona, "onto the others."

Within the span of five minutes, Rona had picked the locks of all but three of the cages. Non-Trons big and small were prancing delightedly around the hot room, relishing their newfound freedom. Galaen was elated; he felt as if there was a gigantic bubble of happiness inside of him.

Suddenly, Rona shrieked. Galaen whipped around and saw a gigantic figure looming over her, casting her lithe frame in shadow. Seeing it, the non-Linear's fur stood on end. It yowled and raced towards the door, but the figure pulled something out of a holster and pointed it at the small non-

Tron. "No!" Galaen screamed, and the figure turned to face him. Seizing his chance, he cried, "Rona, run!"

Rona jumped up and aimed a blow at the bulky shadow's head, but it swatted her away as if she were a fly. She crumpled to the ground, and the figure turned back to Galaen. Seeing that the nonTrons had escaped, he shouted, "Do your worst!" His only hope was that he could buy enough time for Rona to escape.

The figure pointed the object at Galaen, and something clicked deep inside of it. Galaen tried to dodge, but a bolt of white light flashed — and everything went black.

***

Galaen woke. He looked around groggily at his surroundings. His eyes were blurred, but even through the haze, he recognized that he was in an unfamiliar place. He tried to stand but found that his limbs were tightly tied to a pole. Whoever had done it had been meticulous; they had left no room for Galaen to move. As a result, he hung limply about two feet off the metallic ground.

Suddenly, Galaen was jarred by a rattling sensation. The pole was being shaken by what felt oddly like turbulence. He glanced up and saw an enormous black-haired man clad in navy blue robes looming over him. Galaen was jolted again, but this time with a surge of recognition. This man was the figure in the cage room who had threatened the nonTrons, who had incapacitated Rona, who had shot him with a stun gun and tied him up.

"You!" Galaen screamed, shaking with rage and terror. "What did you do with Rona?"

The man chuckled. "Who? Spare me the unpleasantries, child, I have no time for your bratty whining. I am Zurn, High Officer of the Watch, and it has come to my attention that you are meddling in affairs best left to adults. As such, you shall be duly punished." The man grinned evilly. "We of the Watch are dedicated to protecting the population, you know. And then you come along and free those vulgar animals. They will destroy us if left unchecked! In fact, the entire reason we have prospered for so long is that we eliminated them the first time! And now… they're back."

Zurn pretended to shudder, then straightened up. "But never fear! There is an upside. You will be present at their total annihilation!" Zurn laughed darkly, a terrible sound that chilled Galaen to the bone. Then he was gone, and Galaen slumped in his bonds. This was terrible. When they arrived at whatever safe haven the non — animals had found, it would be blasted to bits. But with what?

The answer came to him all too soon. The feeling of turbulence, the implication of heavy weaponry — Galaen was in an airship.

The gigantic, artificial beasts of the sky served as army vehicles, even though the colonies hadn't needed armies since before Galaen was born. For the first time, he was glad his history Program at school had drilled the formerly useless information into him. But if it truly was an airship and — Galaen glanced around, trying to determine its size — a big one at that, then the animals were almost certainly doomed.

Just then, someone tapped his shoulder. Galaen glanced backwards and saw an armor-clad figure behind him. Probably one of Zurn's cronies, he thought. The unknown person glanced at him through slits in their helmet and said in a muffled voice, "Don't try to resist. I don't like it when prisoners resist. It makes me want to... blow something up."

Galaen gasped. "Rona?"

"In the flesh," she answered. Galaen looked closer and saw a tuft of chestnut hair sticking out of her helmet. It was her, and better yet, she had somehow come to rescue him."Now, let's get you outta here."

In less than a minute, his bonds were cut. Galaen slumped to the floor with a sigh of relief, and Rona did the same.

"How did you get here?" he asked.

"After Zurn knocked me down, I slipped behind the cages, then tailed 'im all the way here," she answered. "After that... Well, it's easier to use a stun gun than you might think."

Galaen was a little baffled, but he decided to go along with the answer. "And what do you plan to do to get us out of here?"

"Hmm," Rona murmured. We could — watch out!" She shoved him to the ground as a beam of light shot past them. There, with his stun gun still smoking, was Zurn. Rona fumbled with a concealed pocket, but Zurn ignored her, holstering his gun while glaring at Galaen.

"I am almost sorry it had to come to this, boy, but I am about to eliminate an annoyance that is threatening the entire world — and I don't mean the animals," Zurn hissed. "Goodbye, and don't bother me again." The huge man lunged, and Galaen thought he was attacking. But instead, Zurn reached towards a small button on the ship's side.

As his meaty finger pushed the small red contraption, Galaen was struck by a feeling of dread. There was a mechanical whirring from deep inside the ship — and the floor seemed to disintegrate. Galaen felt like he was hanging in empty space for a moment. But all too soon, gravity took hold. The last thing he saw was Rona's anguished face staring at him from the hole in the ship, screaming words that were lost in the swirling gray mists of Galaen's doom.

    ***

Galaen was consumed not by a rush of fear, but a surge of disattached curiosity. What's going to happen, he thought, after I die? Will Rona stop Zurn? Will the animals be killed? The thoughts drifted lazily through his consciousness, seemingly unaware of the imminent destruction of their mortal shell.

Suddenly, Galaen burst through the clouds. The world was vibrant, brightly colored — almost unnaturally so. Galaen heard an unfamiliar roar that couldn't have come from a machine and grinned. They were here. Good or bad, the outcome of Zurn's scheme was about to show itself.

All of a sudden, he felt a jolt. Galaen looked downwards and saw, not the ground rushing to meet him, but the shining brown feathers of an abnormally large animal. It was one of many he and Rona had freed in the lab. It cawed, and Galaen was struck by a feeling of giddiness. He wasn't going to die!

The creature drifted slowly towards the ground, seemingly defying gravity. As soon as they were near the earth, Galaen leaped down. He landed on soft moss and stood, glancing around. He was surrounded by animals, each and every one of them from the lab. There was a cacophony of roars and caws, the animals seemingly jubilant that he had survived.

Just then, Galaen noticed a small, furry face peeking out from behind a larger animal. It was the non-Linear. "It's you!" he cried, scooping up the animal in his arms. "You escaped!" The creature purred like an engine and rubbed its soft face against him. Galaen felt overwhelmingly happy as he stroked it.

All of a sudden, a metallic crackle filled the air. Galaen's head whipped upwards to identify the source — and saw the airship. The crackle was coming from a small appendage; he assumed it was a loudspeaker.

A voice boomed, making Galaen jump. "GALAEN! THIS IS FOR YOU!" He recognized it instantly.

"DIE!" Rona screamed, and it took Galaen a second to realize she was shouting at Zurn. Through the speaker, the sounds of a scuffle blared, followed by a heavy thud. "GOODBYE, KILLER!" Rona yelled.

Suddenly, there was a loud blast from the airship itself. Galaen looked up just in time to see the airship crumble as it was ripped apart by several gigantic explosions.

Galaen couldn't process the destruction for a moment, just staring as the first bits of ash drifted down. The non-Linear mewled softly in his arms, and he cradled it unconsciously. Only after a moment of stillness did he react.

"RONA! NOOOO!" Galaen sobbed, almost in convulsions. "Why? WHY?" The non-Linear meowed again, and then scratched him.

"What are you doing?!" he yelled, tears dripping down his face. "Rona is dead! Why can't you just leave me alone!" The little animal seemed to shake its head. At the same moment, there was a loud thump.

Galaen looked up. There, on the ground, was the gigantic flying animal. And on its back was... but it couldn't be!

And yet, it was. They hit the ground in an embrace, Galaen laughing while tears streamed down his cheeks. "Whaddya know?" Rona chuckled. "I really did go blow something up!"

And for the first time in his life, Galaen was truly happy.

About the Author

Evan Kaltz is twelve years old and loves to write. He lives near Grand Rapids with his family and many pets, including two cats, a hamster and his own fish tank. He plays piano, percussion and bassoon. He can also be found running cross country, playing D&D, reading or playing video games with his siblings.

Youth Published Finalist

The Hero of the Tales
Vivienne Ostoich

It was a pretty October afternoon when a twelve-year-old boy by the name of Arthur stormed up the stairs to the apartment he shared with his mom and dad. His black hair was caked with that day's lunch, and his designer shoes were stained with mud. Arthur tore the door open, threw his backpack on the floor and plopped on the couch. Arthur's mind wandered through the events of his disastrous day. He'd been late to class, got an F on his history test, and got caught in the middle of a food fight, which is why tater-tot casserole was plastered like drywall over his scalp.

Arthur's frustration had boiled like a volcano while he stood in line to get on his bus. But laying there on the couch, he decided there was nothing he could about it now, so he picked himself up and shuffled to his room. He snagged a well-worn book from the shelf and sat on his bed, making sure not to disturb Tigress—who he had called Tiger until she had had kittens—from her nap before opening the book. Arthur stared at the cover page. It was called The Real Fairy Tales, and it still sent a shiver of excitement up his spine. Arthur's favorite story was about the genies. In that story, the author explained that genies—one of the realm's most powerful creatures—don't live in lamps or pots, but in geodes. They also live in houses that are invisible to their enemies. Arthur was about to peel the pages open when the doorbell rang.

Arthur sighed, put the book down, and went to check the door.

"Here you are, Asher! Your mail." Mrs. Beanpole—their next-door neighbor who could never remember Arthur's name—held out his family's mail.

Arthur— annoyed that he'd been interrupted from his book— grunted his thanks before shutting the door. He then rifled through the mail.

"Bill, bill, junk, bill, and—what?" At the bottom of the pile was a small package about the size of a baseball. It was tied with twine—or was it thread?—and it pulsed like a heartbeat. Excitement and curiosity gripped

Arthur and his hands shook as he untied the knot. Arthur's excitement sparked as he recognized the geode sitting in his palm.

"Is this what I think it is?" Arthur turned the rock in his hands and found some writing scratched on the side. As he ran his finger over them, something on the side clicked, and Arthur heard some sort of melody. Suddenly, the geode flashed brightly. Arthur shielded his eyes and dropped it. The glow faded, but Arthur could still hear the melody—like somebody dropping glitter from a bucket. He peeked through his fingers. His heart leaped in his throat as he tried to process what was in front of him. It was a girl—if you could call her that—with deep indigo skin and shimmering purple hair woven into a tapestry of a braid.

"Valenna, how many times do I— Wait, who— Where am I?" The girl looked around, her red and gold dress swishing with every twist. Catching sight of Arthur (who had attempted to blend into the couch cushions), she grinned. "Aha! Maybe you can explain what's going on!"

Arthur squealed.

Giada sighed. "Let's do this properly. I'm Giada, and you are?"

"Arthur. Wh- What are you?" Arthur managed to squeak.

To his surprise, Giada started laughing. "You're joking, right?"

When Arthur shook his head, she asked, "You press the doorbell on a genie's geode, and you don't know who I am?" Giada again started laughing.

"Genies aren't real, and everybody knows that." Arthur stubbornly responded.

"Well, maybe not in your country, but in the Realm of Stories genies are as common as grass and just as real." Giada smirked.

"If so, show me some magic," Arthur blurted.

"Like what?"

Arthur's mind spun before landing on a single thought. "Take me to the Realm of Stories."

"Okay, your choice." Giada said, popping her knuckles.

Suddenly, the melody Arthur had first heard grew louder as blue mist enveloped him and Giada. When he stopped spinning, everything had changed. They were in a lush forest with a purple brook babbling over some rocks.

Giada jabbed a thumb at the river. "Pei-pom juice. Try some, it's really good."

"Where... am I?" Arthur asked.

"Uh. The Realm of Stories. The place you asked me to take you." Giada smirked. "This is Opposite Woods where everything is backward— Hey! Get out!"

Arthur stopped walking into the river. Thrusting her hand out, blue tendrils snaked their way to Arthur and yanked him back to Giada.

"That side is Antagonist Land," Giada said.

"Antagonist Land?" Arthur repeated.

"Yea, like goblins, witches, vampires, ghouls, mummies. You get the point."

Arthur shivered, and Giada stared into the fog like she expected something to appear. When nothing happened, she turned back to Arthur and said, "This here is Protagonist Land."

Catching Arthur's confused look, Giada explained, "Centaurs, fairies, wizards, dwarves, and fairy godmothers. Protagonists are the good guys while the antagonists are the bad guys."

"Hey, what are genies, then?" Arthur asked. He spun slowly, trying to take in the forest.

"Genies, ogres, trolls and sorcerers can be good or bad, depending what side they choose," Giada explained.

They walked around for a while, drinking pei-pom juice from empty acorn shells the size of a cat. Arthur thought it tasted like tropical punch. After a while, Giada pulled a small pocket watch out of thin air. She flipped the lid and studied the face for a moment, then snapped it shut.

"What'd you need the time for?" Arthur queried, wondering where she'd kept the watch hidden.

"It keeps track of how much time has passed in the Bookling Realm," Giada responded, turning back to Arthur.

"Bookling Realm?" Arthur asked.

"You know, your world. Listen, I need to bring you back. You've been here almost too long," Giada said.

Seeing Arthur's face fall, Gaida quickly added, "Don't worry. I'll see you soon, I'm sure."

With that, Arthur was enveloped in blue, but this time something warm like a mug of tea was rested in his hands. Then, just as quickly as it had started, it stopped. Arthur was on the sidewalk in front of the apartment building he lived in. The weight in his hand demanded his attention. It was a glass figurine of himself with a note on the bottom. "When your face begins to drop, press the button to come back."

Just then, Arthur heard his mom call. "Arthur! Time to come in!" Arthur's face brightened when remembered that tonight was pizza, popcorn, and movie night. All thought of the figurine and genie and Realm of Stories faded to the back of his mind.

Arthur didn't think much of his experience, until the day before Halloween. After school one day, he burst through the front door, ran to his room, and flopped on the bed. Arthur looked at the little figurine, only to find his face looked like it was made of ice cream that had been left out. He plucked it off the nightstand and punched the button. The figurine melted into glitter which surrounded Arthur and Tigress—who had been in her usual spot—and spun around them. When the air cleared, Arthur noticed that it looked like Opposite Woods, but in a twisted way. Just then, a bush rustled and he heard voices. Arthur jolted to the nearest bush and peeked out. It was two stocky creatures with grayish-blue skin and blank eyes.

"The tear is widening, thanks to her," said the darker of the two in a voice so rough it could grate vegetables.

"She's doing a fantastic job— Hey. What's that?"

Arthur looked in the direction the lighter one was pointing in and saw Tigress. He hadn't realized she had come and, in his hurry to hide, he hadn't thought to grab her. He watched as Tigress suddenly stretched and grew into a tiger, flashing very large teeth. The two creatures backed away and ran into the woods.

"Psst. Back here."

Arthur jumped as a blue snake wormed its way down the tree before transforming into Giada. He didn't realize she had tagged along with them.

"I nearly peed my pants," Arthur whisper-shouted.

Giada wrinkled up her noes and said, "TMI, but we got to go before those goblins come back."

"Those were goblins?" Arthur asked.

Giada nodded, "They're the worst of all the Antagonists. They have been coming in droves since the Tear opened." Giada made some cat-like purrs and Tigress let them climb on her back.

"What's the tear and who was the 'she' the goblins were talking about?" Arthur asked after they started moving.

"Long ago a powerful witch broke through the void that separates this Realm from yours. Then some Protagonists tried to seal it, but it breaks every year. This year, Danica, an ancestor of the witch, is forcing it bigger then ever." Giada stopped for a minute, then continued, "Because this is the hundredth year, a hero will implant the Book of True Story on Climax Mountain, and it will close the Tear forever."

They rode in silence for a few minutes. Then Giada purred. Tigress stopped and Giada turned around to look at Arthur.

"Arthur, I need you to promise me something."

"Okay," Arthur said, raising his eyebrow.

"If I ever start turning red or chanting, I need you to run."

"Why?" Arthur asked.

"I don't want to explain it. Just remember to run." Giada finished.

With that she meowed to Tigress and they started again. Arthur mulled over Giada's words, hundreds of questions bubbling up as he looked over the landscape. He hadn't realized it, but they had left the Woods and were in a rolling pasture with grass waving in the air.

Suddenly, Tigress stopped and Giada slid off, prompting Arthur to follow. Tigress sat down and started grooming herself while Arthur followed Giada through the meadow. Strangely, she kept making odd turns like she was avoiding something. Arthur wondered if she was dodging traps. Suddenly, Giada stopped, raised her fist, and pounded the air three times.

Arthur jumped at the sound, then remembered something from his book. "This is genie protected, right?"

Giada turned and said, "You can't see it? Oh, that's right, you're a Bookling."

Just then he heard a door creak open before Gaida sent blue mist over his eyes. Arthur fanned the air and saw a giant castle. A hand reached out from the doorway and beckoned them in. Giada raced inside and Arthur was quick to follow.

"Welcome, Arthur, I've been hoping you'd arrive soon," said an old lady as she opened the door.

Arthur stared at the lady. "Mrs. Beanpole?" The lady and Giada laughed as his cheeks grew warm.

"In the Bookling Realm, yes, but here I'm Mother Hubbard." Then she bowed and said, "Welcome, Hero of the Books."

Arthur looked at Giada, who looked as confused as he felt.

"Come, I will explain," Mother Hubbard said. She walked down a hallway which led to a small room with plush chairs and a roaring fire.

After they were all seated, Giada piped up. "I told him the legend of the Hero of the Books and the Book of True Story."

"Oh, good. Arthur, I've been keeping watch over you for a long time. I gave you the package in hopes Giada would bring you here. Now you must place the Book of True Story in Climax Mountain."

"But how?" Arthur burst out, standing up. "I can't climb mountains, I'm scared of heights, and I'm no hero."

Before Arthur could say more, Mother Hubbard said, "You are honest and have courage even though you don't realize it." She gently but firmly sat him back down. "Besides, who said anything about climbing?" With a twinkle in her eye, Mother Hubbard whistled and a carpet came flying down the hall.

"Hey, rug! Long time no see. Are you here to help?" Giada asked.

The carpet twisted around Giada as she giggled.

While they were playing, Mother Hubbard said, "The carpet will get you and Giada up the mountain. Oh, by the way, here's the Book of True Story." With that she handed Arthur a book.

"Wait, I can't go with Arthur," Giada declared, "It's too close to the goblins."

Mother Hubbard sighed and walked over to Giada and whispered something in her ear. After a pause, Giada nodded.

"I got it!" Arthur interrupted, smacking his palm on the arm of his chair, "I thought this looked familiar. It's The Real Fairy Tales!"

"Yes, the book goes into the star on top of the mountain," Mother Hubbard responded.

She gave Arthur and Giada a few more instructions, and then they were on their way. After the first couple of tense minutes flying on the carpet, Arthur began to relax and peeked over the edge at all the places below as Giada described them. There was Sweety-town, where everything was made of candy, Bookburrow, which was an underground library, and Dwarf District, which had plenty of hills and rocks because (as Giada explained) dwarves are really a crossbreed of centaurs and gnomes so they love climbing. They also look like baby centaurs with beards.

Arthur snickered at the description, then looked up to see Climax Mountain towering before them.

"Watch your step," Giada said in a hushed tone as they stepped off of the carpet.

"Are you okay?" Arthur asked. He noticed that Giada had gone pale.

Giada jumped, and then said, "What? Oh yeah, I'm okay."

Arthur didn't push. "It doesn't look like anyone's here," Arthur said quietly.

Just then, half a dozen goblins and a terrifying, yet beautiful woman popped out of thin air.

"Well, hello, Hero," said a goblin.

"Or should we say, ex-Hero?" laughed another.

"Ah, Giada, we meet again, my friend," said the woman.

"We are not friends, Danica," Giada retorted through gritted teeth.

"We'll leave that for another time. Now, Hero, give me the Book," said Danica, turning to Arthur, her eyes burning holes in him.

Fear coursed through him, but a calm trickle of—something—overcame the fear. With determination in his eyes, Arthur firmly said, "No."

"Fine then, if you won't give it to me, I'll take it!" Danica barked orders to the goblins, "Get them, but don't kill them or hurt the book."

The goblins rushed toward them as Giada gathered mist into a ball. Then, the ball transformed into two short swords. She started swinging them wildly at the goblins.

"Arthur, get the book to the—Argh!" Giada dropped the swords and grasped her head, shaking it. Arthur watched in horror as red streaks snaked up Giada's arms. The goblins stopped and started snickering as Giada dropped her arms and turned to Arthur. Her eyes looked like Tigress's when she saw a rat. Giada started towards him. Just then she lunged. Arthur rolled to the side as the goblins cheered.

Arthur watched as the red spread toward Giada's face. He heard her mutter, "Fear. No. Fight it. I can't—"

Just then, a breath of wind passed by them both. Arthur could swear he heard it say the word courage.

Giada froze, then lifted her head to the sky as the red began to fade away. Tilting her head back, Giada roared, "Courage!" The word echoed off the mountainside like a lion's roar. Forming two new swords, Giada turned back toward the goblins, knocking them left and right.

"Go to the star! I'll cover you!" Giada shouted. Arthur looked into her eyes which were clear and strong.

Following Giada, Arthur ran through the goblins. Whenever there was trouble, Giada was there. Just as Arthur made it to the star, Danica screamed and shot a ray of red light at him, but Giada stopped it with a beam of blue.

"Arthur, place the book," Giada yelled over her shoulder as she pushed Danica's magic. Arthur fumbled with it, nearly dropping the book, then shoved it into a groove in the star. A shockwave tore through the air, knocking Arthur off his feet. He hit his head on a rock. He heard a ringing noise and then everything went black.

"Tigress, stop licking me," Arthur mumbled as he came to. Tigress was still tiger size, so Arthur's whole head was wet. Rubbing his eyes, Arthur sat up and saw Giada. He was in the room he had been in Mother Hubbard's castle.

"How are you doing?" Giada asked.

"I'm not sure," Arthur responded. Suddenly, everything came flooding back.

"What happened? Where's Danica? Is everything all right?" he said, sitting up.

"Whoa, slow down. Yes, everything's okay. Danica evaporated when you placed the book in the mountain," Giada explained. She went on to tell him the Tear was closed and all the Antagonists went back home.

"Why did you turn red on the mountain?" Arthur wanted to know.

"Truth is, I'm half goblin," Giada calmly responded.

While Arthur processed that bombshell, Giada went on, "I was always afraid that I'd hurt someone until I faced my fear," Giada smiled, "Mother Hubbard had told me about courage before we left, and it helped me break through."

Just then, Mother Hubbard and two other people walked in.

"Arthur James Grey, are you okay?" one of the figures asked.

"Mom, Dad, is that you?" Arthur was suddenly enveloped in arms, with tears everywhere and questions flowing.

"Wait, how are you here?" Arthur asked.

"This might be a surprise, but you, Dad, and I are wizards," Arthur's mom replied.

"D-does that mean...I'm a wizard?" When his parents nodded, a realization dawned on him. "So are we staying here?"

"Yes, you will go to wizard school and live right in this town near Giada."

"All right!" Arthur shouted, pumping his fist in the air. Just then, his stomach growled. "Can we get some food first, though?"

About the Author

Vivienne Ostoich loves to read. From modern American histories to high fantasy, she devours anything with pages. She enjoys making up stories, telling them to her four younger brothers and sisters and living them out with her friends. She was born in Texas but lives with her family in Kentwood, MI.

About Write Michigan

The Write Michigan Short Story Contest began in 2012 as a dream. Kent District Library Director Lance Werner envisioned libraries and publishers working together to highlight the efforts of Michigan writers via an independently published book.

Since then, Write Michigan has become a celebrated annual event that invites Michigan residents of all ages to showcase their storytelling talents. Organized by the Kent District Library and Schuler Books, the contest aims to foster a love for writing and provide a platform for local authors to gain recognition. Over the years, it has grown in popularity, attracting hundreds of entries each year from aspiring writers across the state.

Participants are divided into three categories: youth, teens, and adults, ensuring that writers of all ages have the opportunity to compete on a level playing field. The contest features a rigorous judging process, with entries evaluated by a panel of experts as well as through public voting. Winners in each category receive cash prizes and the honor of having their stories published in an anthology by Chapbook Press, which is available for purchase at Schuler Books.

The Write Michigan Short Story Contest not only celebrates the art of storytelling but also builds a vibrant literary community in Michigan. It offers various writing events and workshops throughout the year, including the popular Days of Learning, which provide valuable resources and support for writers. The contest has become a cornerstone of Michigan's literary scene, inspiring countless individuals to share their unique voices and stories.

2026 Judges

SUSIE FINKBEINER

Susie Finkbeiner is the author of *The All-American, All Manner of Things* - both of which were selected as Michigan Notable Books - *The Nature of Small Birds* and *Stories That Bind Us*, as well as *A Cup of Dust, A Trail of Crumbs and A Song of Home.*

When she isn't writing, she's spending time with her husband and three kids or performing at her local community theatre. She lives with her family in West Michigan.

Find her at Facebook, Instagram, and BookBub.

JENNIFER FURNER

Jennifer Furner has been published in *HuffPost Personal, The Rumpus, Belt Magazine* and others. She is a past fellow of the Kenyon Review Writers Workshop and currently serves as the Nonfiction Editor for *The Dodge,* an online magazine of eco-writing. She lives in Grand Rapids, Michigan with her husband and daughter. For more of her writing, visit jenniferfurner.com.

A.H. KIM

A.H. (Ann) Kim is the author of the novels *A Good Family* and *Relative Strangers,* both published by Graydon House/HarperCollins. Educated at Harvard College and Berkeley Law School, where she was an editor of the California Law Review, Ann worked as a corporate lawyer for many years in the San Francisco Bay Area before deciding to retire early and move to Ann Arbor. Ann is proof that you don't need to be an English major or have an MFA to be published and that it's never too late to start. More information about Ann and her writing may be found at www.ahkim.net.

SOPHFRONIA SCOTT

Sophfronia Scott is a novelist, essayist and noted contemplative thinker whose work has earned wide recognition, including a 2020 Artist Fellowship Grant from the Connecticut Office of the Arts and the 2021 Thomas Merton "Louie" Award for her book *The Seeker* and *the Monk.* A native of Lorain, Ohio, she holds degrees from Harvard University and Vermont College of Fine Arts. Her career began in journalism at *Time* and *People,* where she co authored the influential "Twentysomething" cover story, the first major study identifying Generation X. Her debut novel, *All I Need to Get By,* garnered acclaim and a nomination for best new author at the African American Literary Awards, with Henry Louis Gates Jr. calling her "potentially one of the best writers of her generation."

Scott is the bestselling author of *Wild, Beautiful, and Free* and has written several other books spanning fiction, essays and spiritual reflection. Her work has appeared in publications such as *Yankee Magazine, The Christian Century, North American Review* and *O, The Oprah Magazine,* with multiple essays recognized as Notables in *Best American Essays.* A sought after speaker and workshop leader, she has presented for organizations including the Episcopal House of Bishops, the International Thomas Merton Society and the Glen Workshop. She is the founding director of Alma College's low residency MFA in Creative Writing and lives in East Lansing, Michigan, where she is pursuing a PhD in Creative Writing at Bath Spa University.

JANYRE TROMP

Janyre Tromp is an award-winning book editor by day. By night, she spins deliciously suspenseful historical novels that, at their core, hunt for beauty, even when it isn't pretty. She's the best-selling author of *The Scorpion Thief, Darkness Calls the Tiger, Shadows in the Mind's Eye,* and *Lovely Life* and co-author of *O Little Town.* And that all happens from her unfinished basement when she's not wrangling all the things-including her fantastic teens and crazy fur babies.

You can find her as @JanyreTromp across all social media platforms and her website, www.JanyreTromp.com (where you can grab a free copy of her novella Wide Open).

Acknowledgments

Over the last fourteen years, the Write Michigan Short Story Contest has helped authors share their stories with the world.

We extend our heartfelt gratitude to the esteemed judges of the 2025-2026 Write Michigan Short Story Contest: Susie Finkbeiner, Jenny Furner, Ann Kim, Sophfronia Scott and Janyre Tromp. Your dedication and expertise have been invaluable in selecting the outstanding stories featured in this anthology. We are also deeply honored to have Kenneth Kraegel as our Keynote Author, whose insights and inspiration have enriched this year's contest.

This anthology would not have been possible without the generous support of our sponsors: Schuler Books, Meijer and Kent District Library. Your contributions have helped us nurture the creative spirit within our community and provide a platform for local writers to shine.

Thanks also to the Write Michigan Committee for tirelessly organizing, promoting and bringing fun to the contest: Brad Baker, Amber Elder, Keeva Filipek, Randy Goble, Janice Greer, Josh Mosey, Lauren Hagerman Tekelly, Deb Schultz, Remington Steed and Katie Zuidema.

Lance Warner, Executive Director of Kent District Library, and Bill and Cecile Fehsenfeld, owners of Schuler Books, have been steadfast champions of this project since day one.

Our appreciation goes out to artist Adolfo Valle for providing us with the beautiful Write Michigan artwork. May the stories within this firefly-bound book shed light on your own stories. See more of Adolfo's work at adolfovallestudios.com.

We are immensely thankful to the public who submitted their stories, sharing their unique voices and perspectives. Our heartfelt appreciation goes out to the volunteers who tirelessly read and evaluated the entries, ensuring a fair and thorough judging process. Finally, we express our gratitude to the readers and buyers of this anthology. Your support not only celebrates the talent of local artists but also helps sustain a vibrant literary community in Michigan. Thank you for being a part of this creative journey.

Josh Mosey, Kent District Library
Pierre Camy, Schuler Books

Sponsors

SCHULER BOOKS

meijer

Schuler Books
Self-Publishing Services

Thanks to Schuler Books' Espresso Book Machine, we can help you print your book. You provide us with two PDF files (one for the cover and one for the text or bookblock) and we will print a high-quality paperback book for you, in color or black and white. The Espresso Book Machine can print books from 40 pages to 650 pages long.

What are the benefits of printing your work with Schuler Books?

- This is your book.
- You'll receive one-on-one support
- Since you sign a non-exclusive contract with us, you may pursue any other publishing venture that you choose.
- You retain all rights to the printed work, and you have complete control over layout, content and design.
- No minimums. You may print one copy or as many as you want.
- You retain rights for non-exclusive distribution and may sell books printed at Schuler Books or with the Chapbook Press through any avenue.
- Modifications are allowed at any time, for an additional fee.
- You set the book price and determine the royalty per book.

What we need to print your book

2 print-ready PDF files: one for the book and one for the cover, formatted the way you want them to look. We will upload your files and print a paperback edition of your book on high quality (archival) paper and a full-color glossy cover, in any size you want from 5"x 5" to around 8" x 10.5"

We can help you get there

We can help as much or as little as needed in each area of making your book a reality.

New Services:

- e-Book /Global distribution print and digital package: Your title (in print or as an eBook) will be available for purchase to over 39,000 global retailers, and their customers. The eBook will be available for more than 70 different

Ereaders including Amazon Kindle, Apple iBookstore, Barnes&Noble NOOK, Kobo, Sony, etc.) Bookstores and retailers around the world will be able

to order your book for their customers.

- Title set-up:
  - Book and e-book: $520 (includes 2 ISBNs)
  - Book only: $420 (include 1 ISBN)

You need to order a minimum of 50 copies within 60 days of title set-up. Additional orders (minimum quantity of 10), require a three week notice.

- Epub Conversion: $0.80 per page (page

count is based on the total number of pages in your bookblock)

  - Conversion will take three weeks.
  - For Printing costs and author

compensation please ask for a quote.

Chapbook Press

Chapbook Press	Short Run	Standard Package	Chapbook Press Publishing
	$50 Plus Production Costs	$150 Plus Production Costs	$300 Plus Production Costs
Maximum Print Run	20 Copies	Unlimited	Unlimited
Page Maximum	100 Pages	650 Pages	650 Pages
Personal Consultation	30 Minutes	30 Minutes	60 Minutes
Email Support	Limited Support	Included	Included
PDF Review	No	No	Yes
Proof Copy	1 Proof Copy	1 Proof Copy	1 Proof Copy
PDF Upload	Includes initial upload No Re-uploads	Includes initial upload +1 Re-upload	Includes initial upload +1 Re-upload
Cover	Basic Text Cover	Basic Template Cover	Basic Template Cover
Saved for Re-prints	No	Yes	Yes
ISBN/Barcode	No	No	Yes
Library of Congress Reg.	No	No	Yes
Books in Print Reg.	No	No	Yes
Sale: Schuler Books	No	No	Yes
Sale: SchulerBooks.com	No	No	Yes
Production Costs	$7.00 per copy flat rate	$6.00 per copy +$0.03 per page	$6.00 per copy +$0.03 per page
Color Interior	No	+$0.15 per page	+$0.15 per page

A la Carte Sevices
PDF alterations (re-uploads): $25 (+ price of proof copy)
Scanning: $50 deposit / $50 per hour
File conversion to PDF: $5
Cover from template: $50 (prepay)
ISBN & barcode acquisition: $100
Amazon listing: $50
Library of Congress Registration: $50
Additional consultation time: $40 per hour
Additional PDF adjustments: $60 per hour

Freelance Fees
Pre-press file consulting: $15 per 1/4 hour
Manuscript evaluation: $250
Manuscript editing: $135 deposit, $45 per hour
Proofreading: $105 deposit, $35 per hour
Transcribing: $105 deposit, $35 per hour
Coaching: $50 deposit, $50 per hour
Custom cover design: $100 deposit, $50 per hour
Page layout: $100 deposit, $50 per hour
Hardcover Binding: Ask for a quote.

For more information visit SchulerBooks.com
Want to talk to someone? Call us today at 616-942-7330 x558,
or email us at: printondemand@schulerbooks.com